To Charlie —

Have a
great adventure!

Jason Edwards

Will Allen
and the
TERRIBLE TRUTH

Chronicles
of the

VOLUME FOUR

The Adventure Continues

in this fourth installment in
the *Chronicles of the Monster Detective Agency* series.

In volume one, *Will Allen and the Great Monster Detective*

Timid middle school science whiz Will Allen is plagued by
monsters. Fortunately, he learns how to conquer them with the help
of the Great Monster Detective, Bigelow Hawkins, and his very
special monster-fighting tools: the RevealeR and the MonsterScope.
Bigelow then recruits Will to become a monster detective himself,
and together with his friend and partner, Jeannine Fitsimmons, he
starts his own Monster Detective Agency.

In volume two, *Will Allen and the Ring of Terror*

Will sets out on his first case as a monster detective. But when his
client, Timmy Newsome, is tormented by a monster that appears to
Will to be no more than a harmless golden ring, Will must rely on
the perceptiveness and insight that only his partner Jeannine can
provide. Together they reveal the monster's true form, and save
Timmy and themselves from a horror beyond imagining!

In volume three, *Will Allen and the Hideous Shroud*

Will and Jeannine go off on separate adventures. Jeannine makes
short work of meek Gerald Hoffsteadtler's Banshee, while Will is
stymied by the shrouded monster of star football player Duncan
Williams. But Will's biggest challenge isn't that his client is nasty
or that 'Dunk' and his friends bully meek kids like Will and
Gerald: it's that his monster-fighting RevealeR has suddenly become
more dangerous than the monsters themselves!

And now for volume four...

For information regarding permission, write to:
Rogue Bear Press, P.O. Box #513, Ardsley, NY. 10502
ISBN 10 :   0978951263
ISBN 13 :   9780978951269

Library of Congress Catalog # 2014948264

READING LEVEL RATINGS :

This book is rated **level III** in the **Rogue Bear Press** *AcceleReader* Program.
It is designed for children 8-15 years of age.
Flesch Kincaid reading level 3.9, Lexile 710L, CCSS 2nd - 3rd grade
Learn more about our *AcceleReader* Program at **RogueBearPress.com.**

<u>Teachers and Librarians take note:</u> Rogue Bear Press offers FREE ebook copies and provides discounts of up to 50% on hardcover and paperback editions to schools and libraries.

For details about our discount programs or to be notified about free ebook availability, contact program Director Jan Silverman at <u>Programs@RogueBearPress.com</u> or check out the SEEDING for READING page at RogueBearPress.com

Also inquire about our acclaimed, interACTIVE enrichment programs for schools and libraries:

Will Allen and the
TERRIBLE TRUTH

Jason Edwards

Rogue Bear Press
New York

To Jenna and Jessica,
**wishing you the courage
to follow your dreams**

Books by JASON EDWARDS:

Contents

Chapter 1 - Provocations

Okay, no matter who tells you otherwise, and this means *you* Timmy Newsome, I am a cheerful, optimistic kind of guy. Not that I dot my i's with hearts or draw little smiley faces when I sign my name like my best friend, Jeannine Fitsimmons, but I do try to look at the bright side of life. On the other hand, there have been times lately when that bright side has been hard to see, like when the feelers of a giant squid wrapped themselves around my head and were smothering me to death. So, try though I might to paint a happy picture, let's face it - even if you have a disposition that's sunnier than Miami in June, performing a job like mine is not a barrel of laughs. The work is nasty, the hours are tough, the pay stinks, and on top of it all, the kids you help are sometimes one step up from being a horse's butt. And not a very *big* step up, either. But that's life when you run a monster detective agency.

Mind you, Jeannine loves it. Now don't get me wrong: she's a great friend and a straight-A student like me, not to mention a fine monster detective herself, but sometimes I wonder about that girl. Just last week, she limped home from a case with her clothes in tatters, her mouth bleeding, and covered in scrapes and monster slime, and yet she was smiling like she had spent all night at an amusement park. In fact, lately she seems to enjoy everything she does - even *homework*. If I could bottle whatever happy juice she's drinking, I'd make a fortune.

"Oh, Will," she gushed as we sat together in the musty old broom closet that doubles as our school's computer lab, "we are just the luckiest two people in the world!" As she spoke, Jeannine's fingers danced up and down the keyboard, moving lightly because they were not weighed down by her usual assortment of gothic skull rings. In a flash, the words, "The Case of the Egregious Elephant," appeared across the top of the title page. She leaned in close to the screen to review the other pages she had written, and then uploaded the file to our 'Monster Detective Agency - Solved Cases' folder.

"*Lucky*? How do you figure?" I asked.

"Why, we have it all, don't we?" she said.

I looked up from the math homework that I was supposed to have done two days earlier. Very little of what I saw beside me was typical of the Jeannine I've come to know: no black leather jacket, not a single item of clothing

2

that was hand painted, hand trimmed, or tie-dyed, no paper clips on her ears, and most notably, no combat boots on her feet (for which my toes, which she frequently stomps on, were thankful). With her layered tank top covered by an oversized white shirt, ankle-length stretch pants, and hair pinned up by a huge black bow, she looked like a fashion model - from the 1980s. In spite of my grateful toes, I scowled at her. But in a cheerful kind of way.

"Have it all? Define '*having it all*,' if you please."

Jeannine squinted, and made a sour face at me just like Timmy Newsome's harpy had done when I shined my magical RevealeR flashlight in its eyes.

"Well for starters, ever since the new term began we've got lots of new friends..."

As if on cue, a pair of squeaky-voiced girls called out, "Hey, Jee-Jee!" from the hallway. Both wore pink satin jackets that covered outfits identical to Jeannine's. She waved at them as they passed.

"See?" she continued. "And we both have nice homes, happy families, and good food to eat."

"You call what my mom makes *food*? Have you ever tried her Ox-tail Stew?" But Jeannine would not let me sidetrack her.

"We have our own rooms," she went on. "Our own computers and televisions, and now I've even got an iPhone. And we get to fight monsters! What else *is* there?"

I don't know about you, but my nose twitched from the smell of faulty reasoning. Or maybe it was from the odor of the tofu and roasted pepper sandwich coming from my lunch bag, I'm not quite sure.

"Who are you kidding?" I grumbled. "Maybe lots of people act nice to you now that you're a big movie star..."

"I am *not* a movie star," Jeannine shot back reflexively,

3

though a sheepish smile slipped out as she spoke. "One role in a hit movie doesn't make you a star. I wasn't even the lead."

"…But just because people say hello to you in the hallway," I continued as if she hadn't spoken, "it doesn't mean that they're your friends. Not one of your 'new friends' actually hangs out with us. And you may have your own television, but with all the rehearsals for your new play, plus the private lessons and learning centers your mom sends you to, you never get to watch. You're even so busy that you never showed up last Saturday to help fight Tasha Plitnick's monster! I called your mom to ask where you were, and she said you were 'otherwise engaged'."

Jeannine shrugged, and then sighed, "Well I was. Anyway, it's not like you weren't able to handle it on your own."

"You know that fighting girls' monsters is tricky for me. You said you would help!"

Jeannine didn't answer. Instead, she inspected me up and down, scanning my sneakers, trousers, and Chicago Cubs sweatshirt as though she was searching for some hidden thorn jabbing at me.

"My, aren't *we* in a snit today?" She said loftily. "Just so you know, whoever told you that you look cute when you're cranky was lying."

"I am not cranky!" I shouted.

"Right, not cranky," Jeannine said calmly. "But in case you hadn't noticed, you just crumpled up your math homework."

I looked down at my hands. Both were balled into fists that held crushed bits of the paper I had been writing on.

"Hand cramps," I said. "Doesn't prove anything."

"Really? Well, your cheeks are turning red, like they always do when you get angry."

"Too much sun," I replied.

Jeannine rolled her eyes at me. Let me tell you, if she was looking for something to *make* me act cranky, that would certainly do the trick. She then reached down and gently pulled one of the paper scraps from my hand, smoothed the crumples, and pointed at the writing. It was filled with doodles of screaming faces, ghastly grimaces, gnashing fangs, and decapitated heads.

"That..." I mumbled. "That's just...um..."

Okay, she had me.

"All right, fine! I'm cranky!" I admitted. "I'm in a bad mood, okay?"

"So then tell me why," Jeannine coaxed. "Maybe we can do something about it."

"There's nothing you can do," I said. "I just woke up on the wrong side of the bed or something."

"No, that's not it," she stated firmly. "You haven't been yourself for days. Something must have happened to set you off like this."

She was right, of course. In our time working together, Jeannine has proven herself to be a really good detective. And I'm not saying that just because she kept me from getting eaten alive by a harpy at Timmy Newsome's house.

"Well," I bit my lip, and began stomping at some dust bunnies under the table. "I...I guess maybe I'm just tired of being an underground success. I mean, I know that some kids might be embarrassed about having to hire us to save them from a monster in their closet, but that's no excuse for how they treat us after. None of our clients even want to be *seen* with us once we solve their cases. We put ourselves in danger and get bruised and bloodied to help them, but then they act like they don't even know us."

"That's not true," Jeannine countered. "Why, Glenda Olivieri talks to me in Social Studies all the time now, and she always picks me to be on her team for dodgeball. And Timmy Newsome has had me over to his house lots of times. And Martha Curran…"

"Wait - " I sputtered. *What?* Say that again?"

"Glenda Olivieri always…"

"NO, not that. The part about you and Timmy?"

"We hang out at his house all the time."

"You do?" I gagged, and shook my head like I had been smacked with a brick. "Is it…I mean, are you two *dating*?"

Jeannine's face turned bright red.

"Well, actually, I'm tutoring him in English," she said coyly. "At least, that's what his mother is paying me for."

"Well, maybe I should have tutored him in math, instead of just pretending to do that so his mom wouldn't know what we were really up to. Then he might still have some use for me, too."

"Oh, please," Jeannine scoffed. "It's not like you have much use for him either."

"But it's not just Timmy, it's *all* of them. Jamaal. Amy. Gerald…"

"Oh, now *there's* a big loss," Jeannine said, her nose twitching as if she smelled my mom's asparagus dumplings. "It's not like you'd want him fawning all over you like he used to do to *me*."

"And then there's Erwin Newley," I continued. "Remember him?"

"The Case of the Sinister Scorpion?"

"Um, yeah, I suppose you could call it that. Is that the name you gave the file?"

"It has a nice ring to it, don't you think?"

"I guess so. Anyway, after my RevealeR shrank his monster down to thimble-size and I locked it in his terrarium, Erwin decided he wasn't going to pay me!"

"That's awful!"

"Yeah, and he was pretty smug about getting away with it, too, until I told him I would make it grow gigantic again, and throw in a monster tarantula too."

"Oh, Will, you didn't!"

"I *can't*, but Erwin didn't know that. He paid up in a flash, but now he avoids me when we pass in the hallways."

Jeannine frowned, and began chewing on one of the purple strands of her hair. Some people think that's gross, but I actually like it, because dying a purple streak in her hair and chewing on it is one of the few truly Jeannine-like things she still does.

"Well, it's not like we do it for the money, anyway," she said.

"I know that!" I growled. But I didn't say, *so what **do** we do it for?* Instead, I finished by complaining, "But it would be nice to be appreciated a little."

"Well, *I* appreciate what you do."

"You have to," I answered. "You're my partner."

"That's true," she agreed. "Oh! That reminds me Will: don't forget that you're due at Rhonda Peevely's house at..."

"Six o'clock," I finished. "And I know it goes against nature, but would you mind not being such a nag?"

"Don't you dare call me that!" Jeannine shrieked. "I am not a nag!"

"Who are you kidding? You nag me all the time!"

"I don't nag," she huffed indignantly, "I *remind.*"

"That's not what you call it when your mom does it to *you*."

7

"That's different."

"Really? How, exactly?"

"It's not nagging when I do it to you because you *need* it."

Jeannine is my best friend. When I get older, I'm getting myself a dog.

At 5:30pm, the murky atmosphere blanketing our town was already darkened. I was at home in my room, munching on some week-old popcorn while staring out the window at some blood-red streaks splattered across the dreary mists floating overhead. As the sun crept behind the mountains to the west, a sudden chirp from the alarm on my watch drew my mind back from the clouds.

"Let's get on with it," I announced to the Albert Einstein

poster hanging loosely from my bright blue walls as I tuned and headed over to the closet. My stomach growled as I tossed the bag of popcorn onto my desk beside the half-eaten granola bar I'd snuck up to my room, which lay hidden in plain sight among the mounds of books and papers strewn all across the top. I had rushed through my dinner in order to have time to prepare for my date with…well, whatever it was that awaited me in Rhonda Peevely's room, so I began getting ready by throwing on the bowler hat and beaten-up old trench coat that serve as my monster detective uniform. The proud silver badge on the jacket gleamed brightly as I polished it. I then filled my pockets, as I usually do, with my monster-spying magnifying glass, the MonsterScope, and my truth-revealing, monster-shrinking flashlight, the RevealeR. Those two tools, plus my wits and bravery, are all I've ever needed to solve a case, but this time I reached for one extra item anyway. I grabbed my camera from the shelf and tucked it into an inner pocket of my coat.

At that very moment, hackles arose on my neck and my back stiffened. I can't explain it, but ever since I became a monster detective I've developed some kind of sixth sense, and I knew without a doubt that I was no longer alone in my room. A monster was present. Instinctively, I reached for my RevealeR, but it was already too late.

"Don't bother," a harsh voice whispered. "That can't help you."

Chapter 2 - False Impressions

A monster detective has to rely on his instincts, and in that moment mine drove me to whip around and point my RevealeR at the source of the voice. My aim was dead on target, and even though it was not dark in my room, the RevealeR's strange, fizzy green light cast a stark shadow on the wall as it caught the monster in its powerful beam. I squinted briefly from the glare of the light reflecting off of the diminutive figure, but then I sighed, and lowered my RevealeR.

"Bigelow," I whispered.

For there before me, big as life (or in this case, big as a *Wizard of Oz* munchkin) was none other than my friend and mentor, Bigelow Hawkins, the Great Monster Detective. He was sitting on my bed, completely cloaked, as always, in his oversized trench coat and bowler hat, casually munching on my popcorn. His furry, paw-like feet hung off the end of the bed like a child's.

"Hello Will," he spoke in his squeaky, gravelly voice. "I apologize for startling you, but I must tell you that it won't do you any good."

"My RevealeR?" I held up my flashlight and examined its faded red casing. The raised etchings along the side tingled where they pressed into my hand. "But you told me that as long as I power it with understanding, the light of truth *always* works."

"No, no, I meant your camera," he said. "I'm afraid that it will be of no use."

"Oh, *that*," I grumbled. "That's not to fight the monsters with. It's just that Jeannine and I have been keeping a record of our cases, and I want to start taking pictures for…for our files."

"I'm sorry Will, but you can't," Bigelow said. "Creatures born of the mind can only be revealed with the mind."

Now, in case you hadn't noticed, Bigelow has an annoying habit of speaking in riddles. Or just plain gobbledygook. Most of the time, I patiently try to work out what his arcane messages mean. But this wasn't one of those times.

"Translation please." I hissed.

"Put simply, monsters cannot be photographed."

"What? Why not?"

"Truth, like beauty, is in the eye of the beholder, Will. Everyone and everything sees its own truth. The camera sees *its* truth, and you see yours. But the camera's truth does not include monsters."

"But... but that's impossible!" I exploded. "Everyone can't have different truths. There's only *one* truth! And the truth is: I fight monsters! I find them, I uncover their secrets, and I conquer them! And if I could show people that..."

Suddenly, I realized that I was shouting at Bigelow. And worse, I realized what I was really shouting about. I deflated, and turned my gaze to the window.

"If people out there knew what I've done," I whispered, leaning over the sill and looking out at the twilight-blanketed street, "I'd be cheered as a hero, instead of being treated like a pathetic little dweeb all the time. Don't I deserve that?"

"Of course you do," Bigelow said sympathetically. "But it is not possible for others to see what you've faced. Even those who are right next to you do not, because their truths are different."

"I don't understand."

"No one ever sees exactly what another person sees, Will. Everyone sees things differently. Our eyes, our minds, and our perspectives are all different," Bigelow explained. "That is why it is so difficult, and yet so essential for you, as a monster detective, to try to see from another person's point of view. That enables you to *understand* the monsters they see, so that you can help conquer them. But you never really see what they do."

"What are you talking about? Of course I see what they do! Even without the MonsterScope, I see their monsters as clear as day!"

"Do you? Do you really?"

"Of course I...wait. Are you telling me that I don't see what I *think* I'm seeing?"

12

Bigelow scratched his head. If you know me at all, you know that got under my skin.

"Do you remember the first time you saw another person's monster?" he asked.

"Of course," I replied as my thoughts drifted back. "It was Timmy Newsome's ring monster. And I saw that monster perfectly well."

"But it didn't scare you like it did Timmy and Jeannine, did it?"

I shook my head, and Bigelow nodded knowingly.

"That was because you didn't see what they did. To you it appeared to be a ring, but what they saw was one of their worst fears come to life. Who knows what that actually looked like to them? What you feel changes how the monsters appear to you."

My brain whirred like an old blender, and I fell back against the wall. I began to say something, but then stopped and thought things through for a minute. It was a lot to take in.

"So then," I finally replied, "the monsters can look completely different to me than they do to other people?"

"They look like what you *make* them look like. What does fear look like to you?"

"Hmmm. That depends on my mom," I answered. "Today it looked a little like meatloaf."

Rhonda Peevely's house was down on Cherry Tree Lane, about two miles from mine, so I rode there on my bike - the one I got from Duncan Williams as payment for helping him with his shroud-monster. The thing is, the bike he gave me was one of his old ones, and was a bit beaten up, so I've been fixing it up for weeks. That very day, I had spent over an hour cleaning and painting over

13

some rusty spots. Not that I'm complaining mind you, because this bike was still a big improvement over my old man-eating bicycle, but unfortunately, the last coat of paint that I had brushed on hadn't completely dried when I set out that night. I realized that when I arrived at Rhonda's house and discovered dark blue stains on the inner thighs of my pants where they had rubbed against the frame.

"Oh, great," I grumbled as I got off my bike and examined the wet-looking streaks. "It looks like I just…"

Okay, I am *not* going to say it. I quickly checked my watch, but it was too late to go home and change. Trying to wipe the stains off had no effect: the paint clung on stubbornly. I paced around outside the house for a minute, trying to think of something else I could do. My eyes darted about, occasionally glancing up at Rhonda's house, which glared back at me as if sensing my uneasiness. Its eyes - yellow lights set in the windows at opposite ends of the door, and the colorfully painted moldings and windowsills, made it look like a cross between a gingerbread house and a Jack 'O Lantern. As I watched, a bleak shroud fell across the roof as the last bit of sun dipped behind the mountains guarding the horizon.

"Great," I grumbled. "It's a minute before six, my pants are a mess, I'm about to walk into a spooky version of Hansel and Gretel's house, and on top of it all, I have to deal with a *girl*. This is a party just waiting to happen!"

Honestly, even without stained pants, I wasn't looking forward to ringing that doorbell because I always seem to have much more trouble solving cases that involve girls' monsters. Maybe that's because girls themselves are so much harder to solve. Rhonda, for instance, asked for my help by leaving me a perfumed note in my locker. You'd think she was inviting me to tea or something.

14

When I finally knocked on the door (at precisely six o'clock, of course), a woman with a middle-age size body stuffed into a teenage-size tennis outfit answered it, calling out in a sing-song voice, "Who's theeerre..." as she opened the door. A halo of bleached-blonde hair was pasted around her heart-shaped, orangish face, highlighted by swollen red lips and angular, painted-on cheekbones. Surrounding the bright colors of her cheeks and mouth, waxy skin stretched tightly around her eyes and lips like an overinflated balloon. One glance at me in my ratty trench coat, stained pants, and bowler hat, and she gaped like she was looking at a compost heap dropped on her steps.

"And what can I do for you?" she said, closing the door as she spoke. "If you were hoping to use our bathroom, it looks like you may already be too late."

I gazed down at my stained pants.

"It's paint," I said.

"Of *course* it is," she said.

"I'm Will Allen," I announced. "I'm here to see Rhonda."

"See Rhonda about what?" the woman asked.

"I'm her tutor," I said. But just then...

"Will!" I heard Rhonda call out excitedly from inside. The woman turned back to look at her.

"It's all right, mom," I heard Rhonda say from somewhere behind her mother. "Will's here to practice with me. He's my new dance partner."

Her mother turned back and scoped me with an even more unflattering expression. The leathery skin of her unnaturally tan face almost cracked where the frown lines formed.

"This?" she said disgustedly. "*This* is your dance partner?"

"It's very hard to find a boy who likes to dance," Rhonda explained.

"You must have been desperate," her mother said.

"Oh, yes," Rhonda agreed.

"If you're both *quite* through," I snarled. "Can I come in now? We really should get to work. I have a nine o'clock curfew."

Rhonda's mother grudgingly stepped aside and let me in. But just as I was almost past her...

"Just a moment," she said, stopping me with her hand. "I thought you said you were a tutor."

"Well, um...I am..." I stuttered. "But I'm a boy of many talents."

"I see. Well if you really are a dancer, why don't you show me a nice pirouette?"

I glared at her, but before I could say anything, Rhonda burst out with, "Now mother! Don't embarrass me in front of my partner! And I'll thank you not to be poking in on us, like you did when I had my *last* dance partner over. He never came back!"

"All right, all right!" her mother relented, and let me pass. "Just keep it down up there. I'm having my bridge girls over and..."

"Oh, don't worry," Rhonda said irritably. "We won't come and spy on you while you're gossiping about the neighbors."

"Rhonda!" was her mother's red-faced reply.

"Oh, please, don't try to deny it. Come on, Will, let's go." And she led me up to her room.

"Dance partner?" I protested once we were alone. "Did you really have to say I was your dance partner?"

"Sorry," she said, blushing slightly. "It was the best idea I could think of. You don't think I should have told her what you really do, do you?"

"No," I grumbled. "She'd probably have called a mental hospital, judging by the way she was looking at me."

"Well, it's no wonder! You're a mess! That awful old coat and hat should go right in the trash! And you should get changed out of those dirty pants. I have some dancer's tights in my closet..."

"Don't even think about it!" I growled. "*You* can wear a tutu if you want..."

And right then I looked carefully at Rhonda for the first time since I arrived. She was the spitting image of her mother, but for being fair-skinned, less-wrinkled, and more...ah, *well-rounded*.

"Come to think of it, what *are* you wearing?" I asked.

Now, I'm no fashion expert, but in my book, Rhonda

17

was dressed inappropriately. She wore a fancy pink dress trimmed with satin and white lace, and had her highlight-streaked gold hair all done up with bows and ribbons. It looked like she was ready for a debutante ball, not a monster hunt.

"Why, this old thing?" she said, smiling strangely. "Well, I've always been taught that you have to make yourself presentable when you have company coming over."

And with that, she opened the door to her room, and I stepped in and glanced around. Let me tell you, if there was an instruction book for how to decorate a room for a ballerina princess, this would be the cover photo. For one thing, the space was huge - surprisingly so considering that the house appeared rather small from the outside.

"Wow," I marveled. "Your parents must have opened up the entire upper floor of the house to make this room."

Rhonda nodded. "And the attic too," she said glowingly, waving her arm into the air. Adding to the sense of spaciousness was a vaulted ceiling that rose above the tall, four-post bed, and an adjacent open area with a balance bar on the wall and dance mats instead of carpet covering the floor. The furniture and decorations were spotlessly clean and perfectly matched: the drapes, picture frames, dressers, bedding, and even the trash can were all pink and white, and covered with frills and doilies. The bedposts were patterned with climbing vines that matched the wallpaper, and the bed frame was a swirl of painted steel shaped to look like a princess carriage. It was like walking onto the set of a Disney movie.

"This place is very...ah, nice," I said.

"Thank you."

"Your monster isn't Martha Stewart, is it?"

Rhonda let out an exaggerated laugh.

"Oh, no," she said through muffled giggles. "My monster is positively *evil*. You should hear it!"

"You hear your monster? Does it speak?"

Rhonda gagged. She looked down and quietly mumbled, "Yes."

"Well, what does it say?"

Rhonda didn't answer. Instead, she turned and walked over to her bed and sat facing away from the wall. A worn rag doll seemed to call to her from its perch at the tail end of the bed, and she picked it up.

"Look," I said as gently as I could, "I know it's upsetting, but you have to tell me if I'm going to be of any help."

Rhonda cradled her doll gently. Her head shook back and forth, but then she turned and looked up at me with woeful, puppy dog eyes. Her piteous expression made me feel as though I had just smacked her nose with a rolled up newspaper.

Now that I think about it, maybe I *won't* get a dog when I'm older.

Anyway, through pouted lips she managed to get out, "It says...mean things."

"Mean things? What kind of mean things?"

Rhonda's face twisted. Without warning, she chucked her doll roughly back to its place.

"You *know*," she said impatiently. "Things that...that are *mean*!"

"Oh, of course, how stupid of me. It says mean things that are *mean*. But no threats? No screams? No scary noises?"

She shook her head.

"What kind of stupid monster is that?" I grumbled. "Oh, whatever. Let's go find this *mean* monster of yours."

I walked over and turned off the desk lamp, and then headed to the wall switch. Rhonda sprang up from her bed.

"Wait! What are you doing?" she squealed, her eyes widening in horror.

"To track down your monster, I need to turn off the lights."

"No! You can't!"

"Look, Rhonda, I know you're scared, but..."

"It's not that!" she said, sounding annoyed. "I can't have a boy in my room with the lights out! What kind of girl do you think I am?"

"*What*?" I roared, glaring at her angrily. "I...I'm a professional! I don't mix business with...well, with anything else! This is absolutely necessary for me to do my job. So if you want me to help get rid of your monster, it's lights out."

Rhonda folded her arms in front and glared at me suspiciously. Her jaw jutted nervously as she thought it over.

"Oh, all right," she granted. "If that's part of the job."

I rolled my eyes, but then got back down to business and turned out the light. The dark haze lingering outside Rhonda's window flooded the room, sapping the brightness and color from everything within.

"Now where does the voice come from?" I asked.

"Um, I – I can't say," Rhonda answered, her tone turning dark. "It seems to come from all over, really."

"I see. And do you ever *see* the monster?"

"Well, no, but sometimes there are strange shadows moving across the wall over there." She pointed at the wall next to her vanity. "But it's always too dark to make out a shape or anything."

"Hmm. Not much to go on," I muttered. "But at least it's a start. Let me check it out."

And with that, I reached into my pocket, pulled out my

MonsterScope, and began scanning the wall beside Rhonda's vanity. Now, to the naked eye, the MonsterScope looks pretty much like an ordinary spyglass, but the faint green aura surrounding its lens caught Rhonda's eye.

"What's that?" She asked, leaning in for a closer look.

"My MonsterScope," I answered. "It helps me spot monster trails so I can track them down."

"Oh," she said, and then quietly backed away.

As I moved the spyglass slowly up and down the surface of the wall, shadows swirled upon it like living things. The spiraling vines that decorated the fancy wallpaper swayed creepily as the lens passed over them, but there were no glowing footprints or any of the other signs of monsters that the scope usually finds. I moved on to examine her desk, vanity, trash can, windows, and closet, which were horrifyingly girl*ish*, but not weird in any way, unless you count the fact that the bookshelf beside her desk was lined with picture books of Cinderella, Snow White, and Sleeping Beauty. The MonsterScope grew heavy in my hand as I continued scanning, until finally my search had covered the entire room.

"My scope isn't picking up anything," I announced, putting the spyglass back in my pocket and then returning to her vanity. "Are you sure that this was the spot where you saw something?"

"Positive," Rhonda answered.

You might think that it makes no sense, but sometimes I see things better from a distance, so I stepped back from the wall and looked it over again. I still didn't detect anything monster*ish*, but I did notice that the framed pictures posted next to her vanity seemed sloppily arranged, as though someone had thrown them at the wall and they stuck in place.

"Have you been moving things around?" I asked.

21

Rhonda shuddered and replied, "Wha-what makes you say that?"

"Well, everything else in the room is so neatly arranged. But here it looks like…"

I stopped speaking, because at that moment I noticed that in a gap between two of the pictures there were creases in the wallpaper, as though something heavy had been pressed against the wall. I moved in closer, and spotted at the center of the creases a tiny hole where a nail had clearly once been.

"What did you used to have hung here?" I asked.

Rhonda's face turned ashen, and she sputtered, "How...how did you know that something was there?"

"I'm a detective, remember? I figure stuff out."

"Oh," she said, but then her pale expression blossomed with a sudden smirk. "So then have you figured out who put those exploding ketchup packets in your locker?"

My cheeks reddened, and I gave her a fiery glare.

"How did you know about that?" I hissed.

"*Everybody* knows about that," she giggled.

"Not everybody," I retorted. I thought of Jeannine, wondering if I should have told her. "Anyway, let's not get sidetracked. What was on your wall here?"

Rhonda's giggles fled again. Her eyes hid from mine as she answered, "Nothing was there."

"But then what was this…"

"Nothing was there!" Rhonda shrieked. "Nothing!"

It was a lie of course, and an obvious one. In my experience, when a client gets worked up over some detail I've observed it means that I'm on the right track. I could have pressed further, and probably *should* have, but frankly, I've grown tired of struggling to get people to tell me the truth so that I can help them.

22

"Fine," I grumbled, throwing up my hands. "Then we have nothing to go on."

"Well then what do we do?"

"The only thing we *can* do. We wait," I answered. "We wait for the monster to show itself."

Chapter 3 - Distortions

Just so you know, waiting in the dark for a monster to appear is the part of the job I hate the most. That was especially true in this case because Rhonda kept gawking at me, making it hard for me to focus on scanning the room for monsters.

"What?" I finally growled at her. "Why are you staring at me?" Rhonda, who had been leaning in close like she was sniffing for something, drew back and looked away.

"You..." she whispered in a puppy dog voice, "you don't like me, do you?"

"*Like* you?" I answered irritably. "What are you talking about? I like you just fine."

"It's because you think I'm fat, isn't it?" she pouted.

"What? I don't..." I started to yell, but I stopped and gathered my composure. I whistled a deep breath into my lungs, exhaled slowly, and then lightly brought my fingers together. Bigelow taught me to do that to calm myself when confronted with some creature so bizarre and horrifying that I can't think straight. In this case, of course, I did it because... well, actually it was for pretty much the same reason. I closed my eyes and took another deep breath, and then opened them and looked straight at Rhonda.

"Look, Rhonda, I need to concentrate here. I'm trying real hard to help you conquer your monster, so that you can be free of it. Now, is that something that someone who doesn't like you would do?"

"So...you *do* like me?"

I managed to smile, though my teeth were gritted underneath.

"Yes," I hissed. "So now would you mind not staring at me? This job is hard enough without..."

But at just that moment, a moaning sound filled the room. The hackles arose on my neck as the noise grew loud and shrill, but then it tailed off.

"Could that be it?" she asked. "Could that be the monster?"

"Maybe. That, or someone just sampled my mother's Irish Pudding."

Rhonda grimaced, and muttered, "Um, that was a joke, right?"

"If you ever ate at my house, you wouldn't ask," I sighed. "Never mind. I'll check it out." I went to take my

MonsterScope back out of my pocket, but it was stuck. I pulled and tugged, but couldn't lift it.

"What's wrong?" Rhonda asked.

"Scope...stuck in pants..." I grunted as I continued yanking on the handle.

"Here, let me help you with that..."

"NO THANK YOU!" I roared. "I'LL HANDLE THIS MYSELF!" But no matter how much I wrenched and heaved, the scope would not come free. Since I couldn't pull it from my pocket, I tried instead to peel the pocket from around the scope. I finally succeeded in squeezing the opening of the pocket around the wide end of the frame, but even though that got the scope out of my pants, I still couldn't raise it. I looked down and gasped.

"How...How did *that* get in there?"

Because what I found in my hand was not my monster-detecting spyglass, but a large metal dumbbell, which weighed so much that it tilted me over like the Leaning Tower of Pisa.

"What's that?" Rhonda asked.

"Ah, sorry. Wrong pocket," I explained as I hauled the weight over and dropped it on her desk.

"It must be in..."

But when I reached into my other pocket, it was empty.

"Ah, I...That is, it seems..." I offered squeamishly. "It seems that something strange has happened to my pants."

"Well, anyone can see *that*," Rhonda said. "To look at those stains, you'd think that..."

"Not the stains!" I grumbled. "I mean these are...are the wrong pants."

"Oh' I've had that happen!" Rhonda said, suddenly perking up. "I once wore cream colored pants with an eggshell blouse. It was a disaster!"

26

I frowned. Disaster seemed to be the case here as well. Without the RevealeR or MonsterScope, I had nothing to fight the monsters with. So, naturally, that was when...

"Rhondaaaa..." called a deep, ghostly voice that echoed all around us.

"N-No!" she cried. "Oh, no! Go away!"

"Rhondaaaa…it's meeee…." the voice rang out.

"It's here!" Rhonda shouted, shaking my arm violently. "It's here! Do something!"

"I'm on it!" I shouted back, pulling free of her grasp. But without my monster-fighting tools, I was at a loss for what to do as the darkness surrounding us intensified. Shadows crept out of their hiding places and slithered across the floor and up the walls.

"Speak to me, Rhonda," the voice bellowed.

"No! No!" Rhonda pleaded. "Make it go away!"

"I...I..." I stuttered helplessly as a wave of frigid darkness enveloped us. Panic fought to take hold of me as the shadows poked and prodded my body like smoky spears. Ice flooded my veins, and my lungs wheezed as they struggled to draw in the frosty air.

"Breathe," I whispered to myself. "Breathe deep. You can do this." I closed my eyes and focused on inhaling and exhaling slowly. My breaths calmed, and as they did I brought my hands together. Warmth returned to my fingers, and my mind cleared.

I can't fight monsters now, with no MonsterScope or RevealeR, I thought. *What I need is to make the monsters return, for now, to their hiding places. To do that, I've got to turn the lights back on.*

"Rhondaaa…" The echoes bounced all around us.

"Make it stop!" Rhonda cried desperately, shaking my sleeve. "Please, make it stop!"

"I will!" I shouted. My eyes flung open and spotted at once the lamp on her desk, and I lunged over to it.

"This should send you monsters back home for a time out," I chuckled, and then flipped the switch.

But nothing happened. At that moment, a creepy, hollow laugh arose from deep within the shadows crawling up the wall beside me. On top of that cackle, like a layer of frosting on a cake (or in my house, on my mother's tuna casserole) came the haunting voice once more.

"Come now, Rhonda," it called out. "You know you want to play."

"I don't!" Rhonda screamed. "I'll never play with you again!"

"Play?" I gasped. "You *play* with your monster?"

"Aren't you supposed to be doing something!" she shouted back angrily. I blanched.

"Uh, right," I mumbled. "We've got a bit of a problem here…"

But at that very moment, the shadows that had crept up the wall beside Rhonda's vanity began to swirl. At the fringes, a solid-looking border congealed to form a frame around the dark vortex. Then, from deep in its depths, the monster's voice boomed once more.

"Say the words, Rhonda," the voice commanded.

"I won't!" she yelled. "You can't make me!"

"Say what?" I asked. "What does the monster want you to do?"

"I won't!" she insisted.

But then the ghostly voice did it for her.

"Mirror, mirror…" it intoned.

"No! Stop it!" Then she turned to me. "You useless dweeb! Can't you make it stop?" And with that, she dropped to her knees and buried her face in her hands.

"Rhonda, I...I don't understand what's going on."

"Mirror, mirror, on the wall…" the voice continued.

I turned from Rhonda, sobbing on the floor, back to the wall. The border of the shadows had become thicker, and carvings arose along its edges of shells, fish, squids, and other sea animals. The ornate frame, roughly the size of a baseball jersey, floated upward until it was about head high, with the howling shadows still swirling within. Then the surface of the shadows solidified, growing slick and glassy. Finally, a face appeared. Blazing eyes emerged first, and as they intensified, a silver-white skull, ridged and metallic-looking, formed around them.

"Well," I whispered. "At least this bugger wasn't hard to find."

"Who is the fairest of them all?" the harsh voice laughed. Deep echoes of that laughter bounced all around us, but then its tone changed, turning shrill and high-pitched.

"Not you, Rhonda," the piercing voice screeched. "Not you, you fat little pig!"

"No!" she cried, sobbing. "No, don't say that! You can't!"

"Oh, come now," the monster sneered in what was now clearly a woman's voice. "You know that there are no happily-ever-afters for ugly girls."

"*That's* your monster?" I asked in disbelief. "I've had bad hair days that are scarier than this!"

"Help me," Rhonda begged. "Do something!"

"It's not *me* that has to do something, it's *you*," I told her. "Face your monster. Don't hide from it. When you face your monster, it loses its power over you."

"Yes, face me!" the monster laughed. "Face the mirror and take a good, long look!" At that, the skull-like visage in the mirror rippled like a reflection on a rolling pond. It twisted and wriggled, growing swollen and pinkish, until finally a new image formed.

"You have *got* to be kidding me…" I muttered. Rhonda stared blankly at the face in the mirror, and began to cry.

"It…it's…*me!*"

It *was* Rhonda. But even though it was clearly her, the picture was terribly askew, like a fun house mirror. The monster-mirror showed a Rhonda that was bloated and deformed, with a ghastly, swollen face and a pig-like body, ears, and nose. I glanced down at the real Rhonda, crying in front of the distorted reflection, thinking that it was like a scene from a fairy tale gone horribly wrong. That was when it hit me.

"That's it," I whispered to myself. My brain lit up, and in spite of the darkness surrounding me, my vision turned startlingly clear, as though a fog had lifted. "Of course! Who is the fairest of them all? That's it!"

I knelt beside Rhonda, who was still staring, horrified, at the image in the frame.

"Rhonda!" I shouted. "The thing that used to be hung on the wall there...It was a mirror, wasn't it?"

"No!" she cried. "No, it wasn't!"

"It *was*," I insisted without the slightest doubt. This was no hunch or guess - somehow I could *feel* the truth in my grasp as surely as I might hold a cup or a spoon. "And you used to play pretend with it, didn't you? You used to pretend you were Snow White, and it was the magic mirror!"

"H-how? How did you...?" Rhonda covered her face and began sobbing again. Finally she confessed, "Okay, it's true! But then it started to say the most horrible things back at me! So I took it down. But it wouldn't stop! Even without the mirror there, it just wouldn't stop!"

And then she broke down crying hysterically.

"Rhonda," I said gently, leaning down and putting my hand on her shoulder, "It isn't real! That isn't what you look like! It's just the monster, trying to hurt you! That's not you!"

"Oh, but of course it's you," the monster's voice taunted. "Look at it, Rhonda. Look upon your true face."

"Don't listen, Rhonda!"

The eyes of the monster in the mirror turned and gazed up and down at me as if to size me up, but then focused back on Rhonda.

"This…*boy* is a bad influence," the monster snarled.

And with that, the carvings of squids along the edges of the mirror's frame began to pulse. They wriggled and squirmed, and then finally their tentacles sprouted from the surface.

"Oh, NO! NOOOO! Not *squids*!" Rhonda shrieked. "I HATE squids!"

As if beckoned by the terror in her voice, those slimy arms reached toward Rhonda. I jumped in front of her.

"Leave her alone!" I challenged, raising my fists. The monster's face broke into a wide, twisted grin.

"What makes you think it's *her* I'm after?"

And as if to drive home the point, the tentacles wrapped themselves around me and hauled me toward the wall.

"I think it's time we take you out of the picture," the shrill voice cackled. "Or perhaps…put you *into* one!"

The monster pulled me up to the mirror and dragged me in close. I tried to push away by pressing my foot up against the glass, but there *was* no glass. My foot slid right through the surface and into the wall, as though the mirror was a lake, and I was slipping in for a little dip. Biting cold swam up my legs, and as I sank, a harsh laugh echoed from the dark recesses within.

"This picture isn't the real you, Rhonda!" I cried out as I braced my arms against the wall. "You need to see that!"

"Who will you believe, Rhonda?" the mirror droned, "Me, or a little boy who wets his pants?"

"It's paint!" I shouted at the mirror, but then turned back to Rhonda. "Rhonda, you have to listen to me!"

32

But Rhonda was still sobbing uncontrollably, and did not answer.

"Oh, if only I could show you the truth!" I growled. "If only I had my..."

But I stopped, because suddenly there was a familiar burning sensation against my leg. I pushed my free foot against the wall and then dropped my hand into my pocket.

"My RevealeR?" I puzzled as I pulled it out. Its faded red casing and tiny etchings along the barrel were unmistakable. "But a moment ago it wasn't... Oh, never mind!"

I turned and pointed it at the image in the frame, then flicked the switch. The flashlight fizzled and sputtered a bit, but then a powerful stream cascaded out. This was no normal beam of light - it looked more like a river of glowing soap bubbles, many of which were tinted in pale shades of blue, green, and red. But the light was strong and bright, and it made the face in the mirror recoil.

"N-Noooooooo!" The creature howled, and the arms dragging me into the mirror released their grip. I crashed to the floor, landing painfully on my head as usual, but kept the beam focused squarely on the monster. The distorted reflection in the mirror turned gaunt, brown and leathery, then it crumpled and lost its pig ears and tail. Finally, the entire form began to writhe and shrink, and the tentacles retreated back to the frame.

"Fool!" the shriveled visage roared. "You cannot defeat me! This little light will not keep me at bay for long!"

Unfortunately, the monster was right. The only person who could truly defeat that thing was still on her knees, sobbing uncontrollably.

"Rhonda!" I hollered as I ran back to her. "I need you to look! You have to look at it Rhonda."

"No!" she cried. "No, I'm fat! I'm fat and ugly!"

At the sound of that, the monster-mirror swelled again, in spite of my RevealeR's light. It grew even larger than before, until it covered the wall from floor to ceiling. The monster laughed heartily, and then the squid-like arms, now much larger and stronger, shot out from the frame again, grabbing me. I struggled to hold the light steadily on the monster as the tentacles coiled around my arms and began pulling me back to the wall.

"Rhonda!" I shouted desperately, "You're not ugly! You're not fat! Look in the mirror! See the truth about your monster!"

Slowly…much too slowly for my liking, seeing as how I was being hogtied by slimy tentacles and dragged into a typhoon of darkness, Rhonda's eyes turned upward.

"Look at me," Rhonda sobbed. "I'm a lard! A horrible, overweight wretch!"

But to my eyes, the mirror showed a shriveled, brownish skull with bright red lips.

"What?" That's not right…" I growled as my feet reached the wall and were pulled up toward the swirling vortex of shadows within the frame.

Right then I heard Bigelow's voice in the back of my head.

"Truth, like beauty, is in the eye of the beholder," he had said.

I'm not seeing what she sees, I realized. *Whatever image of herself that Rhonda is seeing now is the truth to her. But I need to make her see the truth that I see.*

At that very moment, a sudden burst of heat in my hand drew my eyes down to my RevealeR, which sparked my memory. *Maybe I can do what Jeannine once did. Maybe I can use the RevealeR to show Rhonda a different truth - MY version of the truth!*

34

But even as that thought ran through my brain, my feet slipped and fell sideways into the frame of shadows. Deeper and deeper I sank, and my frantic squirming and struggling did not stop the gigantic tentacles from dragging me even further into the wall. It was clear that I had only one chance. I closed my eyes and tried to imagine a truer, cheerier, happier picture of Rhonda. My mind focused on that vision, and then I opened my eyes and pointed my RevealeR right at the monster's face. Many of the bubbles of light turned bright blue, and were soaked up by the image in the mirror, which began to shimmer. Deep in the heart of that glow, a new likeness formed.

"That picture was just how the monster wants you to see yourself, Rhonda!" I called out. "But look again! Look now and see yourself as *I* see you."

Just then, the coils wrapped around my face, but still I held the light steady. Rhonda looked at me, struggling with the monster, and bit her lip.

"Rh…onda … tr..ust m-me…" I gurgled out as the tentacles grew tight around my mouth, cutting off my air.

"I…I'll try," she said weakly.

Rhonda looked up into the mirror and squinted while I, though my lungs burned and my body was waist deep in the shadowy vortex, tried to keep concentrating on my image of her. White spots flashed before my eyes, and as they faded, my strength faded as well. Blackness closed in, and drowned me until nothing remained.

Chapter 4 - Revisions

My senses, my world, *everything* was being consumed by the darkness. In moments, it would all have been over.

But then…

"Why...why I don't look fat at all!" Rhonda cheered happily at the picture I had projected. "I *am* a pretty girl!"

And with those words, the monster howled, and its grip on me weakened. I used my last remaining bit of strength to pull the feelers from my mouth, and then gasped, gratefully filling my lungs with air. My eyes cleared, and the universe restored itself.

"I do look pretty," Rhonda said, admiring the image in the mirror. "But why am I wearing a clown costume?"

"Ummm…sorry," I panted, as the monster tentacles weakened and I pulled my mouth free. "That's just a wardrobe malfunction. Look again." Then I concentrated harder, this time making certain to keep any stray images out of my mind.

"Why, look at me!" she said, smiling broadly at the image before her, "I'm the belle of the ball! I look like a fairy tale princess!"

I thanked my lucky stars that I remembered watching Cinderella when I was a kid. The monster's grip slackened, and I yanked my legs out of the swirling shadows and tumbled to the floor, landing, as always, on my head. Echoes of rage howled from deep within the mirror - much deeper than the monster on the surface.

"A princess?" the voice from the mirror scoffed "Oh, come now Rhonda, it's time to stop playing childish games…" But then the princess-faced monster momentarily turned its gaze toward me and squealed, "…*isn't* it?"

A crescent-shaped glint appeared in the monster's eye, as though reflecting some small, shiny object. For some reason, I shuddered.

"That voice," I mumbled as I pushed myself up from the floor and rubbed the swelling bruise on my noggin, "That tone of… of *disgust*. It's so familiar."

But though the image looked like Rhonda in a princess costume, it was definitely not *her* voice. As Rhonda and I stared at the face in the mirror, it shifted and deformed, as though it was struggling against the form I was projecting on it. The image rippled from the face of a teenager to that of a mature woman, and then back and forth again.

"You're not going to win any pageants looking like *that*," the monster taunted, its aged face turning brownish and leathery. "It's time to face reality."

A frozen grimace devoured Rhonda's smile, and tears welled in her eyes. Mine, on the other hand, opened wide, because I realized where I had heard that voice before.

"I know who you are," I whispered coldly as the light from my RevealeR intensified, and then I turned to Rhonda. "And so do you, Rhonda."

Rhonda's face turned pale, and a whimper bubbled from her lips. My hand reached out and found hers, and drew her eyes to me. My RevealeR burned like fire, and its warmth flowed through me, and into Rhonda.

"It's time, Rhonda," I said. "It's time to face her."

Rhonda's eyes never left mine, but her head nodded ever so slightly. I nodded back, and then lifted my RevealeR one more time. Its light of truth, clear, strong, and unyielding, burned away the fear and lies that shielded the monster, and its true form was finally bared. A sneer arose from its darkly tanned, leathery visage that was much like the one that greeted me at Rhonda's door.

"You're not a child anymore, Rhonda! You're not some toddler in a tiara! You can't go dressing up like a princess!" the monster crooned. "And would it kill you to eat a salad once in a while? Just look at you!"

"Why, mommy?" Rhonda cried as tears bled onto her pretty pink dress, "Why do you *hate* me so?"

"Your mother doesn't hate you, Rhonda," I said.

"She does!" Rhoda insisted, pulling away from me angrily. "She hates me! You should hear the horrible, hurtful things she says!"

My hand held tightly to hers, and I squeezed it gently. The searing pain deep in her heart passed through our intertwined fingers into me, and I saw her, *really* saw her, for the very first time.

"I once thought the same was true about my dad," I told her. "He was being mean and cranky and I didn't understand why. But I've learned that you have to look past that. You need to see the *whole* truth."

I gazed deep into Rhonda's eyes, and as I did, warmth flowed freely between our hands. At that very moment, my RevealeR pulsed, and a stream of pinkish sparkles joined

its beam. The light burned even brighter, so bright in fact, that the bubbly flow melted together into one intense beam. Bathed in that blinding radiance, the image in the mirror rippled again as its face was swallowed by the powerful illumination. Slowly, the glare faded, revealing a curly blond-haired toddler dressed in a fine ball gown. Her face was painted with more makeup than my great aunt Martha, and draped across her shoulder hung a banner that read 'Little Miss Sullivan County'.

"Thank you! Oh, thank you!" The child beamed joyfully as she was presented with bouquet of roses, and she performed a perfect curtsy as a tiara was placed upon her head. A camera flashed, preserving the moment in amber.

"Is that *you*?" I asked. Rhonda shook her head.

When the glare from the flashbulb faded, the image in front of us had changed to that of a middle aged woman, worn and wrinkled, sitting alone in a musty attic. Tears poured freely from her face as she gazed down at an old news clipping that read, 'Little Girl Wins Big.' The paper was torn and yellowed, with a photograph below the headline that showed the bright, curly-haired girl crowned with her tiara. The woman clutched the photo to her heart, but then looked at her wrinkled hands and cursed their leathery fingers. Then she lifted her other hand, which held a second picture: a much less weathered photo of another ball gown dressed toddler with the same curly blond hair.

"Oh no, Rhonda," the old woman whimpered. "I can't have you end up like me. Not you. You can do so much better. You're going to make something of yourself."

As I stood watching, her pain somehow radiated out and burned its way into me. I looked over at Rhonda, and could sense that she felt it too.

"Mommy," she whispered as her hand went slack in mine, "I...I didn't know." Rhonda took a deep breath, and her eyes sank. Finally, she nodded, and glanced over at me.

"I understand now," she said. I smiled at her, and released her hand.

"Then you know what you need to do."

Rhonda nodded again, then stepped up to the mirror and pressed her fingers to the surface.

"Mom," she whispered. "I...I see you now."

And with that, her hand pushed through the glass-like veneer and reached in to touch the image of her mother. Gingerly, Rhonda caressed the face of the rippling form, and gently stroked its hair. Flares erupted where her fingers fell, and their glow surged through the room. From the shadows hiding among the rafters overhead to the dust bunnies under her bed, the burning brightness permeated everything, including me. A comforting warmth filled my belly like hot cocoa on a bitter day. But what was warmth to me was a raging fire to the monster. It howled, and the swirls of darkness swelled with huge waves as though caught in a typhoon. Then they burned away. The scorching flood of light melted the monster's tentacles to slag, and the mirror shrank in the sway of Rhonda's gentle touch. The monster wailed as the frame surrounding it collapsed, becoming thin and oblong. As it shriveled, the carvings and fancy decorations embedded in the frame aligned themselves along the topmost edge. On the opposite side, prongs sprung out, like fangs growing from a werewolf's jaw. The monster kept shrinking until it was only a few inches long. When its transformation finished, the shrieking suddenly died, and the object fell from the wall, landing behind her vanity. I rushed over to check it out, but I needn't have bothered.

"My comb!" Rhonda exclaimed, leaning down and picking it up. "My beautiful, 'Princess of the Sea' comb! I've been looking for it for ages!"

"Probably ever since you began hearing all those 'mean things' from your wall," I said dryly. "That comb is your monster."

Now, normally I would examine an object with my special spyglass to be sure that it was a monster, but, seeing as how my MonsterScope had disappeared, I had to go on a hunch. And a comb that turned into a skull-faced magic mirror that tried to suck me into swirls of darkness that sank deep into a solid wall seemed a pretty safe guess.

"It is?" Rhonda instantly threw it down on her vanity.

"Don't worry," I reassured her. "Now that you've faced the truth about it, the monster has lost its power over you. It can't grow big and hurt you any more. Just so long as you remember to look at yourself more kindly from now on."

"Like *you* do?" Rhonda smiled at me strangely. "Do you really see me as a...a princess?"

"Uh, well..." I mumbled sheepishly. "More of a duchess, I suppose."

Rhonda moved uncomfortably close. When she spoke, her voice was as soft as a prayer.

"You rescued me. You even jumped in front of those horrible tentacles to protect me."

"Well, that's what I *do*."

"My hero," she murmured. "My brave knight." She leaned forward as if she was about to whisper something in my ear, but then her eyes grew heavy, and she tilted her head so that her lips reached out to me.

At that moment, I did what any other red-blooded American boy my age would do when a girl launches puckered lips at him: I sneezed. I didn't mean to - it was one of those reflex kind of things, but I wasn't exactly disappointed about the fact that it made Rhonda pull back and cover her face. I don't think it was a snotty sneeze, but judging by the way she wiped her face disgustedly, it wasn't exactly dry either. But hey, looking at the bright side (which IS what I do) at least I didn't hurl all over her.

"Rhonda?" a voice called out. "What's going on in there?"

"Your mother!"

"The lights!" Rhonda pointed urgently. "Turn on the..."

But even as she spoke, the door flew open, and in stepped Rhonda's mother. She flicked on the light, and glared at us menacingly.

"Dance practice? In the dark?" she hissed.

"I...umm..." was all Rhonda managed to say. Her mother ignored her, and turned to me.

"Uh, well..." I sputtered, thinking quickly. "We had the desk light on, but just now it stopped working. I think the bulb blew."

Rhonda's mother scowled, and reached over and flicked the switch on the lamp. The light came right on.

"Or, *not*..." I mumbled.

"I think you'd better leave now," she said coldly.

"Yes ma'am," I said, certain that she had no idea how grateful I was to be getting out of there. I stuffed my RevealeR back into my pocket, and then went to the desk to pick up the dumbbell.

"Urmmm..." I groaned as I struggled to lift it. "I suppose you're wondering why I brought this..."

"No, I'm not wondering at all," Rhonda's mother replied.

"*I* am," Rhonda muttered. Meanwhile, I grabbed the dumbbell with both hands and yanked it off the desk, then squirmed and strained to stuff it back into my pocket. Once it finally slid in, it felt surprisingly light. Rhonda then walked me out, her mother eyeing us both all the way. When she opened the front door, I quickly stepped through, hoping to make a clean getaway, but before I could escape, Rhonda tapped my shoulder.

"Could you...maybe come back again?" she asked. "Just to make sure it's gone?"

"Ah, sure," I answered, thinking to myself that between Rhonda and her monster, I considered the monster to be far less dangerous.

One sure sign that it's been a crummy night is when the highlight of the evening is climbing back into your own house through the second floor bathroom window. I had purposely left that window unlocked in order to sneak past my mom before she noticed that I was out past my curfew again. To be perfectly honest, I hadn't even told her that I was going out that night, much less working on a case. She's not a big fan of my adventures, and with my dad out of town on business, there was no one to talk her out of locking me in my room to keep me from setting off on another quest. Believe me, no matter how dreadful monsters can be, they are *nothing* next to my mom when she's on the warpath.

I shimmied up the climbing tree in my back yard and then inched out onto one of the thick branches that stretched toward the roof. Unfortunately, because I'm still a growing boy, the branch was less forgiving of my weight than it used to be. It groaned in protest, and then just as I reached my foot to the shingles, it began to crack. For a moment, I pictured the next day's newspaper headline: "Boy Survives Monsters - Gets Killed Falling From Tree," but I flung myself desperately into the air just as the branch shattered, and bellyflopped onto the roof as the limb crashed into our yard. A light came on in the window below me, and then the inner curtains parted as the top of my mother's head stuck out to inspect the fallen branch.

"Oh my..." she muttered. "What happened here...?" She then turned and looked up at the tree, and I held my breath and pressed myself down against the roof to stay out of view.

At that very moment, a chipmunk scooted along the gutter toward me. It came in close, sniffing me like I was covered in chestnuts. I held steady, not wanting to make a sound, but then the little rodent must have smelled the peanut butter crackers that were hidden in my inner pocket, and decided to go after them. That furry bugger scurried across my hat, right down my face, and into my jacket. To keep from shouting out, I bit my tongue so hard it bled. Meanwhile, my mother must have seen enough, because her head disappeared back into the house, and then there was a loud slam as the window was shut. I instantly rose up and swung myself around until the chipmunk flew from my coat like a cannonball.

"And stay out, you little fuzz ball!" I hissed as it scampered away along the gutter. Unfortunately, my violent movements had caused my feet to slide, and they slipped down and over the edge of the roofline. I quickly grabbed ahold of the drainpipe and stopped my fall just in time. For a moment, I hung there with my feet dangling above the top of the window, clinging to that pipe for dear life, but then slowly I pulled my way back up to the roof.

Naturally, when I got to the bathroom window, it was stuck. As I thrusted upward to try and lift the jammed frame, my feet slid back and tumbled off the roof again. After one more turn hugging the drainpipe, climbing back to the roof, and struggling with the cranky old window, I finally got it open. I stuck my head in and looked around to be sure that my mom wasn't nearby, and then quietly slid my feet in toward the cold tile floor. I set them down and stepped gingerly forward - only to slip on a bar of soap and crash to the floor, knocking over the soap dish, toothbrush holder, and pretty much everything else that wasn't nailed down in the process. I flayed like a squawking duck, grasping the shower curtain as I fell in an attempt to keep from landing on my head. A failed attempt, I might add.

"Oooouuuww! What idiot left soap lying on the floor?"

But then I remembered that my mom had nagged me that very morning about my not having put the soap back in the soap dish, and how it could easily wind up on the floor where someone could slip on it.

Okay, so once in a while she's right about something. Get over it.

"Will!" a tired, and yet shrill voice called out from below. "What going on up there?"

"Ah, nothing," I shouted back. "I'm…um, washing up."

"With what, a jackhammer?"

At just that moment, the shower curtain rod decided it could bear my weight no more. It slid down off the wall, and the rod and curtain collapsed on top of me.

"Will!" my mom shouted. "Are you all right?"

"F-Fine," I stuttered as I struggled to right myself. A pounding beat of anxious footsteps flew up the stairs and down the hallway in my direction, and I knew that if my mom caught me like that I was toast. There was only one thing to do - I tore off my coat and hat and threw them under the fallen curtain, then pulled down my pants and sat quickly on the toilet. When my mom burst though the door, I don't know whose face turned more red, hers or mine.

"MOM! WHAT ARE YOU DOING IN HERE?!"

Let me tell you, she shut that door so fast that she smacked her own head against the frame on the way out.

"What..." she mumbled in a dazed voice, "what happened in there?"

"The shower curtain fell. I'll fix it just as soon as I...as soon as I'm done."

She stayed quiet for a minute, but then collected her wits enough to call back, "Well...well, see that you do!" And then the drumbeat of her steps resumed, and faded down the hallway.

When I finally got back to my room, I sat on my bed and sunk my head into my hands. My eyelids slowly drooped like molasses dripping down a windowpane, and I struggled in vain to keep them open. Finally, as my head began to bob, I kicked off my shoes and tried to lay down, but something in my pockets poked at me. I removed my RevealeR, and tried to get the dumbbell out too, but it was stuck again. I grunted and groaned as I yanked at the handle, but it stayed put as if it were glued in place. I howled in frustration, but then fatigue overtook me, and I succumbed at last, with my hip still anchored to the bed by the overwhelming burden that it bore.

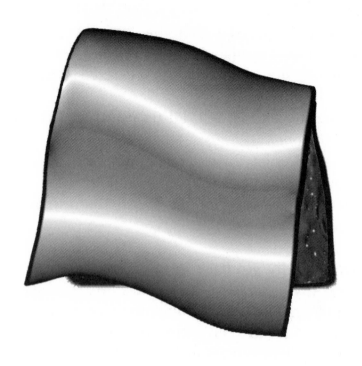

Chapter 5 - Delicacies

My dream brought me back again to that dreadful day. Confronted by the unlikeliest of challenges, my cleverness, wits, and experience had all boarded themselves up in some hidden cavern of my brain, leaving me defenseless. A symphony of cruel laughter filled my ears as I stood frozen in place, helpless to do anything except absorb every bit of the horror being heaped upon me. Suddenly, one cold, demented laugh rose above the others, and in that moment I was flooded with the sensation of eyes boring into me.

"Who...Who's there?" I whispered.

My eyelids fluttered. I awoke, and furiously blinked the fog from my vision, only to find myself nose-to-nose with the image of an upside-down face. Old and pale, with a thick grey mustache and a head covered by tufts of unkept white hair; the flat, creased picture fluttered indifferently mere inches from my eyes. Apparently, some of the tape holding my Albert Einstein poster in place had come loose during the night, and now its top half hung down from my wall, staring blankly at me as it billowed in the morning breeze drifting in from my window.

"Go back to sleep, Albert," I growled, pushing the paper away with the back of my hand. The wind blew it right back into my face, and I rolled over, retreating from those dark, faded eyes.

"There," I muttered. "Now maybe I can get some sleep."

But suddenly my eyes opened wide as a realization struck me: the weight that had pinned my hip to the bed no longer held me in place. I sat up and reached into my pocket.

"Well I'll be..." I breathed.

For there in my hand was my MonsterScope, seemingly good as new, with its faint green aura floating around the lens like a cloud. I examined it carefully, searching for any clue as to what could have made it change form the night before. A switch hidden in the handle. Some magic words etched into the frame. *Anything.* But it looked the same as it always did – like a plain, black-framed magnifying glass with a faint aura around it.

"Come on!" I growled as my head shook in frustration. "There must be *something* here..."

But then my alarm clock began bleating "It's a Small

World After All", so I set the scope down on my desk next to my RevealeR and got up to get ready for school.

As I splashed my face with the warm spray from the bathroom faucet, a jumble of questions rolled around inside my head like a loose marble.

What went wrong with my scope last night? I wondered as I absent-mindedly slathered paste onto my toothbrush and launched it into my mouth. *Did Rhonda's monster somehow cause it to change form? Or is the scope acting weird on its own, like my RevealeR did last year?*

I gasped as a terrible thought occurred to me: *What if the MonsterScope starts spouting fire too?*

Just then, my pondering was interrupted by a fit of retching - it turns out that I had squeezed foot cream instead of toothpaste onto my toothbrush. After briefly cleaning up, and then gargling about a gallon of mouthwash, I made my way down to the kitchen. But even as I sat spooning my mother's home-made granola into my mouth, my mind was elsewhere (which was just as well, because that breakfast tasted like sawdust mixed with birdseed). My foggy daze followed me from my house all the way to the bus stop. The gloom trailed along and settled across the trees lining Everbone Lane, sapping the color from their leaves. When I climbed aboard the bus, Jeannine seemed to sense that something was bothering me before I even landed in my seat.

"Well, you're in another cheerful mood, I see?" she said as I plopped down next to her without looking up.

"I'm fine," I grumbled.

"Really? Then why do you look like you're auditioning for a role as a zombie with constipation?"

"Dunno," I answered in a staunchly casual voice.

"Maybe it's my mom's pork fritters repeating on me again."

"Oh, come on, Will! This whole moody attitude of yours is getting old. If something is bothering you, just say so already!"

"Nothing is bothering me!"

"Fine!" Jeannine growled, and then turned away. She sat fidgeting for exactly seven seconds before bouncing back. "So tell me already! How did it go last night? Did you find Rhonda's monster? What *was* it? Did it have lots fangs? Did it spit fire or slime? How did you conquer it?"

I turned and found her staring at me with a mixed expression of anticipation and exasperation on her face that would do my mother proud. But that was the only thing about her that looked remotely Jeannine-like, because she was once again dressed in one of those stupid, fashionable outfits. Today that meant pink shorts, a plain white t-shirt, and fluffy pink leg warmers over high-top sneakers. But the part that made me cringe the most was the pink satin jacket on top, the same as the one worn by all of the snooty, stuck-up girls at school. The only item that didn't fit in with this perfectly matched outfit was a thick, multi-colored twine bracelet wrapped around her wrist.

"What's this?" I asked, grasping the bracelet between my thumb and forefinger.

"A gift," Jeannine said, pulling away.

"From *Timmy*?"

"Seriously Will?" Jeannine scoffed. "Would a boy give a girl a bracelet made of twine?"

I might, I thought. But I could tell by her tone that it would be the wrong answer.

"I guess not." I answered instead. "So who then?"

"It's a friendship bracelet Glenda made for me. All the girls are wearing them."

"Since when do you wear what everyone else wears?"

"Not everyone! Just the girls I hang out with. And anyway, it's just a bracelet."

"But it's not just the bracelet. Lately you've been dressing just like them. It's like you're turning into..."

"Stop changing the subject! You didn't answer my question. How did it go last night? Judging from the fact that you're here in one piece, I guess you managed to survive without me."

"Everything went fine," I said.

"So, tell me!"

I sighed. "There really isn't much to tell. Rhonda's monster was a bogus magic mirror that told her she was fat and ugly."

"Oh my lord!" Jeannine gasped, clasping her hands to her face. "That's the most horrible monster ever!"

Girls, I thought irritably.

"It was no big deal," I said. "Rhonda comes from a family of beauty queens, and she was afraid that she isn't pretty enough. The monster was feeding off of her self-image problem, so I used that trick you did at Timmy's house, where you used the RevealeR to make him see the images you formed in your head. I pictured Rhonda as a princess, and once I got her to see herself like that, the monster lost its power over her and shrank down to a comb. Case closed. We can type it up at lunchtime."

Jeannine grimaced the same as she did the time she sampled my mom's rutabaga stew. "You see Rhonda as a *princess*?" She asked.

"Oh, don't *you* start too," I grumbled. "What difference does it make how I see her?"

"It makes *all* the difference!" Jeannine insisted. "Don't you understand *any*thing about girls? A girl like Rhonda

52

can only see herself as pretty if she thinks someone else sees her that way. So if Rhonda starts to doubt that you really think she's pretty..."

"...Then she'll go back to feeling ugly and the monster will grow powerful again," I finished. I shrugged, and shook my head. "Well then, what should I do?"

"Just compliment her on how nice she looks from time to time," Jeannine said. "Make her feel attractive. That's what any girl wants."

"Look, I'm no...no *lover*-boy! Why don't *you* tell her how nice she looks?"

Jeannine scowled at me.

"*Really*? Do you honestly think it will do any good, coming from *me*?" she said testily.

I reluctantly shook my head.

"No, I guess not," I grumbled.

"Anyway," she said, "I'm already dealing with *another* head case. Gerald Hoffsteadtler came up to me yesterday. At first I thought he was hounding me again, but as it turns out, he had one of our cards."

"Gerald?" I said, my face contorting like I had smelled a skunk. "Gerald Hoffsteadtler has a monster? *Again*?"

Jeannine nodded.

"Then there *is* justice in the world," I smiled.

"I don't know what you're so pleased about," she said with a frown. "Since *you're* the one who's going to have to get rid of it for him this time."

The smile slipped off my face like a clown on a wet floor.

Yes, I know that's a terrible line, but I'm a detective, not a poet.

"Me?" I protested. "What do you mean, *me*?"

But at that very moment, the bus pulled into the parking lot, and Jeannine popped up out of her seat and left me there, with my mouth hanging open and my last question still dangling out.

Well, even though Jeannine's latest bombshell hung over me like the Sword of Damocles, I wasn't able to catch up to her to find out what was going on until lunch. Sadly, we're not in the same homeroom anymore, and we don't have as many classes together as we used to either, so I knew I'd have to struggle through the morning on my own before I could speak to her. Not that *schoolwork* is any problem – that stuff is always really easy for me, but without Jeannine around, I have a much harder time staying out of trouble. All last year, for example, Jeannine was able to keep me out of the doghouse with my Math teacher, Mrs. McCallister, who treated me like I was a blister on the bottom of her foot. Fortunately, that hadn't been a problem this term because my new Math teacher, Mrs. Moscowitz, was much more fair.

She treated *everybody* that way.

Still, I managed to steer clear of any strife that morning… until my 5th period Earth Science class. But *that* disaster wasn't my fault.

Really.

You see, my Science teacher, Mr. Stines, was a smart, dedicated educator and a truly decent guy – as long as you didn't rile him. The man looked like a cross between a nerd and a pit bull, and had a personality to match. He dressed like a geek, always wearing a pinstriped white cotton shirt, floodwater-length black pants, white socks, black shoes, and thick, black-framed glasses. But his body was built like a WWF wrestler, and so was his temper. The problem was, you never knew what might turn that kindly old Dr. Jekyll into the abominable Mr. Hyde.

"Welcome to our Geography unit, my bright, young neophytes," he said cheerfully as the late bell chimed and everyone pounced into their seats like it was a game of musical chairs. "Now this unit is going to be quite enjoyable. You are going to work together on topography projects, building an entire city by producing a series of three dimensional models from topographical maps!"

A collective groan echoed through the room, and for a second Mr. Stines' eyes bulged a bit, but then his face relaxed and he bellowed, "Oh, now don't be like that. This is going to be FUN!"

"Fun?" a derisive voice drawled. "That's your idea of *fun*?"

Everyone turned to look at the speaker. He was sitting in the very last row, slouching in his seat with his long, stringy legs propped upon the desk and his loafers hanging from his dangling feet. Waves of golden hair drifted across his forehead and drooped down in front of dark, disinterested eyes and a thin, square nose. His jeans, T-shirt, and black leather jacket looked like they were peeled right off of a 1950s James Dean poster, but though his clothes cried out 'I'm a rebel', his self-important sneer screamed of his true nature.

"Seriously, Mr. S., you have got to get yourself an Xbox or something."

Mr. Stines' eyes grew wide and a vein swelled on his forehead, but then he blinked, and his face settled once more.

"Please take your feet off the desk, Mr. Anderson," he growled quietly.

J.T. Anderson, one of the chief spoiled rich brats of our school, sighed, and then lazily slid his feet to the ground. Mr. Stines glared, but then turned back to the class and said, "Now, if one of you wouldn't mind passing out the assignment sheets?"

No one volunteered.

Mr. Stines began to fume. "Ah, Mr. Allen, if you please?"

Well, there you have it: another opportunity for me to earn the ridicule of my peers. But what could I do? I got up and took the papers from his hand.

"Thank you, Mr. Allen," Mr. Stines exhaled loudly.

As I walked down the aisle passing out the sheets, a drawling voice muttered, "Brown-nosing geek."

I stiffened, and my hair stood on end. I quickly turned to the slouching figure of J.T. Anderson and caught the brunt of his sneer.

"Here," I hissed, handing him the assignment sheet, "Have some *fun*. I know *I* will." In response, he shot me a look of such utter loathing that it made my skin crawl. But I didn't care. After finishing handing out the sheets, I returned to my desk and took out my binder.

That was when everything turned *really* sour.

You see, when I pulled out my notebook, the top corner had gooey red splotches on it. I didn't have a napkin or anything to wipe them away with, so I scraped them off on the desk. Unfortunately, some of the splotches has bubbles of liquid under the surface, which erupted when I scraped them, splattering slime all over.

"Eeeuuuuw!" the girl next to me shrieked. "Gross!"

"Mr. Allen!" Mr. Stines shouted. "What in the name of Booker T. Washington do you think you're doing?!"

"I…but I …" I stuttered.

"Looks like little Jimmy Neutron has made another big mess of things!" a drawling voice called out. The entire class murmured it agreement.

"Mr. Allen," the teacher growled (I honestly think I saw steam pour out of his ears like a cartoon character), "I will have a word with you after class. In the meantime – GET

SOME PAPER TOWELS AND CLEAN UP EVERY BIT OF THAT MESS - *NOW*!"

Needless to say, by the time I was done cleaning the desk and floor, while my fellow students snickered and laughed at me, I was *not* happy. Fortunately, Mr. Stines had calmed down by the end of class, so he went easy on me: I didn't get any punishment – just a lecture about exercising better judgment and persevering through adversity, which was probably worse. After suffering through that, and then cleaning myself up in the bathroom, I headed off to get my lunch.

The hum of people chattering in the hallway stung my ears as my eyes darted suspiciously back and forth at the figures lining the bleak plaster and cement block walls. I carefully lifted the latch of my locker door and pried it open, but that caution was much too late: the inner walls were already streaked with the same splotchy red stains that I had cleaned off of my book. I dug my arm into the locker to try and wipe them away, but the stains were a sticky, hardened mass that was impossible to purge. As I stood with my arm squirming deep inside the wall, the sound of chuckling filled the air directly above my head. I yanked my arm loose and quickly turned around, only to bang my nose against the felt of a Ashford Middle School football jacket. Hanging over me was a buzz-cut covered flat, square face perched atop shoulders that were as big as a rhino's.

"Well, if it isn't my old buddy, Truck," I growled as I rubbed my bruised beak. "Long time no see…thankfully."

There in front of me, so massive that his body blotted out the entire hallway behind him, was the lone remaining member of the goons I battled last term. Truck (I don't actually know his real name) stood smirking like he had just eaten a wide receiver for lunch, a smile that made me uncomfortable, especially now that my former client, football star and team captain Duncan Williams, wasn't there to hold his leash.

"Hey, Jimmy Neutron, I heard ya blew somethin' up again? They told me ya looked like the loser from a paintball game. Not that ya didn' awready look like a loser."

I glared at him, thinking, *Yeah, and I'll just bet that YOU had something to do with it, too.* But I was determined not to let him get to me.

"Well, you heard wrong, Truck," I replied heatedly. "There's nothing here for you to gloat over. Now don't you have some poor defenseless quarterback to go stomp on?"

"Not 'til Saturday," he snickered. "Today I got plenty ah stompin' ta go 'round."

And then he clapped me on the back...*hard*, and whistled merrily as he walked away. For a moment, I glowered in his direction, but then I grabbed my lunch, tossed my books into the locker, and headed off to meet up with Jeannine.

Now, I don't know about *your* school, but the Ashford Middle School lunchroom was always a huge, noisy mass of mayhem. Still, I didn't expect that finding Jeannine would be any problem, because even though the landscape had changed since last term, what with 8th graders like my former client Duncan Williams and my former nemesis Jacko McNulty having moved up to high school, most things hadn't changed at all. Chief among these was the fact that the room was still divided up into territories a lot like the old west. Minus the spittoons. There were the usual tables: popular kids, jocks, brainiacs, artsy kids, geeks, and all that. Then there was the table way in the back by the trash cans that me and Jeannine sat at, separate and apart from all the rest. But when I looked for her, Jeannine wasn't there, so my eyes poured over the entire room from one end to the other. Finally, I spotted her standing by the cafeteria doors, chatting and laughing with a bunch of girls who, like her, were all wearing pink jackets.

"Hi Jeannine," I said brightly as I walked up to her. "What's going on?"

For some reason, Jeannine blushed.

"Um, nothing…" she said, looking away and putting her hand over her mouth. The girls surrounding her giggled. The entire troop was dressed in matching outfits like it was a team uniform or something, except for one strikingly pretty blonde girl who was wearing a cheerleader uniform under her pink satin jacket, and had on a pair of long, dangling earrings. I gasped in horror when I recognized who she was.

"Tiffany? Tiffany Wells?" I sputtered, and turned back to Jeannine. "You're hanging out with *Tiffany*?"

Jeannine's eyes scrunched. "Yes. So?"

"You do remember who this is, don't you? This is the same girl who …"

Called you a freakazoid. And a skank. But then I remembered that Jeannine hadn't been on the bus with me the morning that Tiffany had said those things about her. I was about to tell her so, but Tiffany cut me off.

"Well well, if it isn't little Jimmy Neutron," Tiffany hissed scornfully. "What are you doing here among normal people? Don't you have something to go blow up?" Everyone around her chuckled, except for the shortest girl in the group, a pale, dark-haired girl who pointedly looked away.

"Don't call me that!" I growled.

Tiffany and most of her friends snickered, but for some reason the short girl shivered. Her face, which was framed by a curve of shimmery brown hair with a single streak of white, was etched with the shadows of the same haughty expression that Jeannine's usually wore, but for her eyes,

60

which were softer, a little sunken, and darker than any eyes I had ever seen. She turned to me, and her gaze burned through me like there was something big right behind me that she was terrified of. A shiver ran down my spine.

"I know you," she whispered.

Just then, Jeannine saw who I was staring at, and her silly smile slipped. She stepped up to me and turned me away from the group.

"Why don't you get a seat, Will," she said. "I'll catch up."

Well, I wasn't happy about it, but I went over to our table and spread out my lunch. I cleaned off a spot for Jeannine, and then sat munching on some alfalfa sprouts while I waited for her to join me. Finally, I looked back to see what was keeping her, but Jeannine was no longer over by the cafeteria doors. My eyes sought out the table where those girls in pink jackets sat, but Jeannine was not with them. I scanned the rest of the table looking for her, but those pink girls were bookended by a bunch of boys wearing expensive designer clothes, the kind you find at those stores in the mall that look like amusement park rides. And in the middle of them, sticking out like a sore thumb, was the rat-like, freckled face of Gerald Hoffsteadtler. He was wearing the same James Dean-type leather jacket as J.T. Anderson, but unlike his well-tailored mates, his ill-fitting clothes hung like drapes on his scrawny frame. Perched beside him, J.T. and his buddies took turns handing Gerald their homework papers, which he looked over and busily corrected. The way Gerald fawned on them, he might just as well have been peeling them some grapes.

"Spoiled rich brats," I sneered. "Sitting there like they own the place!"

"You shouldn't judge people you don't even know,"

Jeannine chided, appearing from out of nowhere and falling into the seat next to me.

"I know them well enough! They're all the same. Smarmy, stuck-up jerks, every one of them."

"Well, one of those jerks is your next client."

"Speaking of that," I said. "What's this about me helping Gerald? Isn't he *your* client?"

"I just can't fit him in right now," Jeannine said. "You know I'm busy rehearsing with my new theater group."

"Every night?"

Jeannine turned and began picking lint off of her jacket.

"Not quite," she admitted. "But my one free evening, I'm supposed to be tutoring Timmy. His English class is doing a poetry writing unit, and he doesn't know a sonnet from a limerick."

"*Seriously*?! You can't fight monsters because you're busy doing Timmy's homework for him?"

"It's not like that! I don't write anything for him. I just..." For some reason, she began to blush. "...I just teach him how. In fact, Timmy said that I've helped him so much that he's going to write his poem about *me*."

I burst out laughing.

"Ode to Jeannine?" I sputtered through the giggles. "That must be rich!"

Jeannine's eyes narrowed and I pulled my feet away in case she got the urge to stomp on them, but then she tilted her head back and growled, "Well, like it or not, I'm busy, and that means you have to take over Gerald's case."

"No I don't," I insisted. "I'd rather leave him to be eaten by the monsters."

"Will!" Jeannine gasped in her *how could you say that* voice. "You can't be serious! He's got one of our magic business cards. That means we have to help him."

"Why? Why should I do *anything* for Gerald ever again? Don't you remember how nice I was to him last year? When he was desperate for anybody to like him, I became his friend. I helped him. I stood up for him..."

"You called him a booger-covered snot rag behind his back..."

"I apologized for that!" I shouted. "And I made it up to him. I was there when he needed me. I even went toe-to-toe with half the football team to defend him! And now look at him: he'd rather hang out with those spoiled, rich brats than us."

"And he won your precious science award," Jeannine added tartly. "First time in three years you didn't get it."

"Only because I lost points because I was too busy helping Timmy fight his monster to finish my project on time," I grumbled.

"Isn't *that* what's really bothering you, Will? You don't like him because he's smarter than you?"

"He is *not* smarter than me!"

"Look, this is stupid," she finally said. "Will you just agree to take the case already?"

"NO!" I bellowed as my cheeks flared and my body grew heated. "Last year you told me that I couldn't solve Gerald's case because I wasn't understanding enough toward him. Well, I'm even less so now than I was then. You know how I feel about him!"

"Seriously? You were able to put your feelings aside and defend a brutish, bullying football player like Duncan Williams, but you can't do the same for Gerald?"

"Give me one good reason why I should!"

"Let's see..." Jeannine said, looking up and tapping her chin with her finger just like my mom does. "How about...because it's your *job*. Or because, deep down, it's what you really *want* to do - you love being the little hero who saves the day. Or because if he ends up getting badly hurt because you didn't help, you'll never forgive yourself. Or because I'm asking you to."

"I asked for *one* reason." I growled. My cheeks were as red as fire engines, and flames licked the backs of my eyeballs. Fortunately, it was for situations like this that Bigelow taught me me how to calm myself. I closed my eyes and focused on slowing and steadying my breaths. Gradually, as my breathing relaxed, the sensation of a gentle mist settled over me, cooling the flames within.

But then something weird happened. As the fires died, a tingling sensation ran up and down my spine, and my mind was drawn to… well, *feelings* that were floating in the air. Happiness. Anger. Fear. Frustration. Envy. They swirled like dandelion seeds in the wind, and then flooded into me until I began to drown in them.

"So…so many…" I murmured. "Too much…"

Just as I became completely overwhelmed, a sudden, sharp pain struck my foot, and drew my mind back to the ground. I looked down at my shoe, and found Jeannine's heel planted firmly on my toes.

"Well?" Jeannine asked impatiently.

"Huh? What did you say?" I mumbled.

"Welcome back to planet Earth!" she growled, rolling her eyes. "Now, will you do it? Will you take over Gerald Hoffsteadtler's case?"

My body shivered, but the tingling sensation had passed. I glanced around the room, but everything seemed completely normal. My eyes turned back to Jeannine, who was tapping her foot impatiently.

"All right, fine. I'll take the case," I spat. "Just tell Timmy that now he owes *me* a poem too."

Chapter 6 - Entrenchment

As the saying goes, when the going gets tough, the tough get going. Or in my mother's case, the tough start cleaning. The dinner table at my house that evening was like a movie set: perfect in every detail and unnaturally quiet, as if waiting for a director to yell, 'Action!'. The air stank of bleach, the counters and refrigerator sparkled, and the gleam from the polish on the kitchen table made me squint when I looked down at my food. Which, given the repulsive mess on my plate, was probably for the best.

But it was too quiet for my mother's liking, especially

since my father was away. She wandered around the kitchen as I ate, straightening the blinds, smoothing out wrinkles in the kitchen towels, and aligning the forks in the silverware drawer, but the way she kept stealing glances at me, I knew that she had something chomping at the bit to come out.

"So, what's new?" she finally offered as a conversation starter.

"Nothing much," I grumbled as I glared at my mother's version of Shepherd's Pie - made with real shepherds.

"Well, tell me about your day."

"What part do you want to hear about?"

"Oh, surprise me."

I looked up at her as she rearranged the plastic flowers in the table's centerpiece, but when I caught her sneaking another glance at me, her eyes quickly darted away.

"Seems to me we've had enough surprises lately," I said. "Like dad's sudden business trip, for example."

"It's been a stressful time for him," my mother admitted. "What with all of the extra pressure he's been under at work."

"He's not the only one feeling stressed, is he?"

"What do you mean?" she asked, wiping a spilled pea from the table.

"I mean that cleaning isn't the only thing you've been doing, is it?"

My mom stiffened. I reached and turned over her hand.

"Stained fingers. The smell of odor-killing mints on your breath. Making brief detours outside…"

"Cleaning is hot and sweaty work," she interjected. "Something that you would know if you helped out a little more around…"

"You've started smoking again."

66

My mother pulled away. Her mouth opened, but her voice failed. Instead she turned and began straightening the ceramic angels on top of the refrigerator.

"You're too young to understand," she finally whispered.

"What can't I understand?"

"Your father and I have pressures that you've never faced, Will," she asserted. "You can't know what that's like until you experience it yourself. And sometimes we need to do things to cope."

"But the way you're coping is bad for you!"

"I will not be lectured to, young man!" she shot back. I braced for getting my ears singed, but instead my mom straightened a chair, took a deep breath, and continued evenly, "Anyway, I'm more concerned about *you*."

"About *me*? Why?"

"You've been acting very…well, *off* lately. Staying alone in your room a lot. Not talking much to me or your father. Losing your appetite. Those are all signs of depression."

Okay, so I'm not the only one in my house who notices things. But just because my mother showed some detective skills of her own, that didn't mean I had to play along.

"Look, just because you read some psycho-babble article in a parent magazine," I charged, "it doesn't mean that you can psychoanalyze me as a hobby."

"Stop being so childish!" she hissed. "You've been acting sullen for days. Not eating. Moping around the house all afternoon. And now you want to go out tonight *alone*? There must be something going on, and I'm worried about you."

"I'm going to Gerald Hoffsteadtler's house to work on a project! It's not like I'm doing…you know, stuff for you to worry about."

"I don't know *what* you're doing! I just know that

you're troubled, and you're hiding something. And that frightens me!"

I winced as the flame of my mother's emotions seared me like hot knives.

"You and dad say you trust me," I grumbled. "*Do* you?"

A deathly stillness came over us, smothering all but the drip of the kitchen faucet and my mother's shallow, forced breaths. She closed her eyes, then exhaled loudly.

"I do," she sighed. "I just…I just think you need someone to talk to."

Though her voice had calmed, the fear gnawing at my mother burned its way into my chest. But the worst part wasn't sharing her pain. It was knowing that I was the cause of it.

Meanwhile, the peas down on my plate, which were still partly frozen, fought to scramble their way out of the mess of runny mashed potatoes and leftover hamburger meat that they were trapped in. I knew how they felt.

"I…I'm sorry, mom," I said guiltily. "I'm sorry if I've been peevish. I'm just upset about what I have to do tonight."

"That project you're working on with Gerald?"

I nodded. "Gerald used to be my friend back when he was a dweeb, but he's become one of the cool kids, and now he treats me like dirt. So I'd like nothing better than to see him hanging by his drawers from a flagpole, but still I have to bail him out on this *project* anyway."

"I can see how that would be upsetting," my mother said, nodding sympathetically as she spoke. "But is that all that's bothering you?"

"Not exactly. But if I tell you the rest you're not going to like it."

"Try me."

"Okay, well this project requires special, ah…*tools*.

68

Only I'm not sure I'll be able to use my tools because once I put them in my pocket, one of them vanishes and the other turn into a piece of exercise equipment."

Frown lines etched themselves into my mother's face. Her eyes clenched like fists, and she brought her fingers to her lips.

"I see," she hissed. "Anything else?"

"Well, if you must know, I'm also ticked off because my bike peed on me, a mirror tried to eat me, a chipmunk chewed on my nuts, and the one person who could help me with all this is turning pink."

My mother stared at me blankly for a few seconds, but then steam exploded from her ears and she slammed her hands on the table.

"Fine!" she said shrilly. "Be that way!" And then she stormed out of the kitchen.

I sighed. I knew that it was a bad idea to tell my mother about the problems I was having with my job. Family and business just don't mix.

The rapid patter of rain pelting the roof echoed through my room as I crumpled into my chair and dropped my head to the desk. As I sat massaging my temples, a soft hum stroked my ear. I turned in the direction of the noise, only nothing was there, but for my RevealeR. I reached to pick it up, but as my hand drew near the humming intensified, and I hesitated. Gingerly, I prodded the faded red shaft, and when my fingers made contact the RevealeR sputtered, then a narrow beam projected out. It danced across the wall on the far side of the room, drawing lines and creating shapes. But there were no recognizable forms, and before I could make any sense of what I was seeing, they faded away.

What in the world was that? Was the light trying to send me some kind of message?

I straightened, and pulled my RevealeR firmly into my grasp. It pulsed with power, but when I flicked the switch, all that came out was a weak stream of tiny soap bubbles.

"You were right, mom," I whispered, flicking the flashlight off. "I do need someone to talk to." Then I tilted my head back and called out, "Bigelow? Bigelow Hawkins? Where are you?"

"I'm right here, Will. As always," a hollow voice answered from behind me.

And sure enough, on my bed in the spot next to my Teddy Bear, the blanket began to swell, and Bigelow's runty little form arose within.

"Mmmmeerrrrff!" he exclaimed as he struggled with the quilt that covered him. "Stupid blanket!" He pulled himself free and then continued, "So, what seems to be the problem?"

"What's the problem?" I grumbled. "Things are all going crazy, that's the problem! Last night when I reached into my pocket for my MonsterScope, what came out was a dumbbell. A *dumbbell*! And then my RevealeR just up and disappeared. And now when I picked it up it...wait. Wait a second…"

It took a few moments to sink in, but there was something strange about him.

"Bigelow, you look..."

My rant melted as I registered that the furry feet that hung out of the bottom of his trousers had lost most of their hair, and had become petite and swollen like a baby's. The fingers that poked out of his trench coat sleeves were soft, and lacked their claw-like nails. It was as though the monster under that jacket had been replaced by a cherub.

70

"Bigelow!" I said. "Is that you? What happened to you?"

"Nothing, Will," he assured me. "Nothing has happened to me."

"But you look so…different."

Bigelow looked down at himself. He patted his belly, waved his feet, and then held his hands out and inspected them. It may have been a trick of the light, but I'm pretty sure he had polish on his nails.

"I'm not any different," he insisted. "But *you* are."

"*I* am? What's that got to do with how you look?"

"If I appear different to you, it is because you are looking at me differently."

"Bigelow," I growled. "In the last day or so, I've been dropped on my head at least three times. So could you make this a little easier for my poor damaged brain?"

Bigelow didn't even chuckle. He turned away and scratched his head.

"Will, do you remember when I told you that a monster will look different to different people?"

"Yes, my memory is still working fine, thank you very much."

"Well, the *same* person will see a monster differently too, at different times."

"What? How is that possible?"

"People change," Bigelow said simply. "You're different than you were when we first met. You're different than you were even a few hours ago. A different person."

"I'm not!" I protested.

"You are," Bigelow maintained. "Some differences are visible, like the fact that you are a few inches taller than last year, but there are also differences in your thoughts and feelings, and these change how you see things,

71

including me and your MonsterScope. Do you remember how you felt the first time you held it in your hands?"

"I - I felt *great*!" A rush of warmth surged through me as the memory arose. "I was excited, and really proud."

"Did you feel that way about it last night? Was it still a wonderful gift, or was it..."

"...A burden," I finished. The warmth vanished as I picked up my MonsterScope from where it lay on the desk. It was unreasonably heavy. "A *weight*!"

"Exactly!" Bigelow smiled. "It is as I told you: monsters take the form you give them."

"Wait a second, Bigelow! Are you... are you telling me that my MonsterScope is a monster *itself*?"

Bigelow shrugged. "Of a sort. Like the monsters, the MonsterScope manifests something that is within you: in this case, your perceptiveness, your intuition, and your ability to focus and tune out distractions. That is why it appears to you as a lens: something that changes what you view in order to make important things easier to see."

My mind was still two steps behind. I held up my MonsterScope and marveled at it as though I had never seen it before.

"My magnifying glass is a monster," I repeated.

"And your RevealeR, too. It embodies your insight into the world around you. You see it as a flashlight because that is how you define an object that provides illumination when everything around you is shrouded in darkness."

"Monsters," I whispered as I raised my flashlight and looked over its worn red form. I flicked the switch, and this time a faint stream of purple and red light bubbled out. "Everything around me is a monster."

"Not everything," Bigelow said. "Not that horrible green bowtie of yours. No self-respecting monster would ever take *that* form."

"But...but *how*?" I stammered, stumbling down into my chair. "I see these things. I hold them in my hands. How can they change from one thing to another?"

"They change as your beliefs change," Bigelow answered. "What you believe makes them what they are."

"What?" My face scrunched like I had just sampled my mother's spinach lemonade. "That makes no sense! What someone believes doesn't *change* things. Stuff like that only happens in silly pretend games and fairy tales."

"If that is what you believe," Bigelow replied gravely, "then that is what's true for you."

And at that very moment, my RevealeR and MonsterScope went stone cold in my hands. The light from my RevealeR died, and the glow surrounding my MonsterScope faded away.

"My MonsterScope! My RevealeR" I cried. "They're...*dead*! What...What happened to them?"

"It is as I told you, Will," Bigelow said. "Belief makes them what they are. Without your belief in them, they are no more than the ordinary objects you hold in your hands."

I furiously flicked the switch on my RevealeR back and forth, but nothing came out. I peered through the glass of my MonsterScope, but the world looked the same as if nothing was there.

"Okay, okay! I get the point!" I growled, shaking my scope and flashlight in his face. "Now turn these back on!"

"You *don't* get the point," Bigelow maintained. "I didn't turn off your RevealeR. *You* did. Don't you see?"

I was about to yell at him, but something made me stop. I froze like a stone, thinking over what he had said, and remained petrified for a long time before finally speaking.

"So, if I don't believe in their special powers, they don't work for me anymore?"

"Now you've got it," Bigelow smiled.

I lifted my flashlight, but it was now nothing more than a barren shell.

"But I still don't get it," I complained. "I've used this dozens of times. I *know* it works. I've seen it do amazing things. How could I stop believing in what I've seen with my own eyes?"

"That is a question that you, and you alone can answer,"

he told me. "And answer it you must. Only then will the RevealeR's power return."

"But...But I need it back NOW!" I shouted. "I have a case tonight! I can't fight monsters without my RevealeR!"

"That is not true, Will. You solved your last case without the MonsterScope, and you can solve this one without the RevealeR too, if need be. You have within you everything you need to defeat monsters. You always did. But you've come to depend so much on these objects that you've forgotten the true source of their powers."

"The source of their powers? What is it?"

Bigelow smiled, but then turned away.

"You must discover that for yourself," he said. "Find the source, Will, and what you seek will be there waiting for you."

And then he grabbed my quilt and flung it into the air. It floated up above his head, and as it slowly drifted down over him, he vanished.

Chapter 7 - Challenges

Find the source, Will. What you seek will be there waiting for you. Broken echoes of Bigelow's words followed me as I marched into the dreary storm that engulfed the world beyond the sheltered confines of my home. As I travelled down Sutterlow Street, bitter winds tore at my body, but it was the questions gnawing at the back of my mind that shook me more.

The source? What is that? How do I find it?

But while my thoughts drifted, an upward gust struck my face, and my toddler-size Captain Nemo umbrella was unable to fend it off. Cold spray stung my nose and eyes, but at least for once my bowler hat and trench coat served as more than just a uniform. I pulled down the brim of the hat and turned up the collar of my coat, which kept most of my face and neck dry. Through the narrow slit that remained between my collar and hat, I saw the stone gates in the distance that marked the entrance to Kensington Gardens, the development where Gerald lives.

Just then, a silent bolt of lightning lit the night sky like a flashbulb, and for a second, the murky atmosphere turned white. In that instant, all of the concealed forms buried deep in the shadows surrounding me were briefly unveiled. The hackles on my neck arose as phantoms from every nook and cranny lining the road clawed at me, and my head jerked about nervously at every chirp, whine, and scratching sound. I began flicking the switch on my RevealeR, hoping that its light, like a lost puppy, had found its way home, but it remained cold, dark, and empty. Somehow, *I* felt empty too. By the time I arrived, I was about six inches shorter than when I had left home.

Gerald's house was a two-story colonial surrounded by broad hills covered in mini-mansions, which rose behind it like a shadow of death. The roof was smothered by an eerie halo of frigid rain that glistened where the drops had frozen upon contact with the surface. The rest of the house appeared as a silhouette pasted upon a backdrop of hazy fog that loomed across the steep gradient to the rear. As I climbed up the steps to the portico, I passed through that haze and onto the gloom-covered porch.

"Go figure - another stop on the Spook Central Line," I muttered to myself. "Why can't anybody I visit live in a *cheerful*-looking house?" And with that, I rang the bell.

But no one answered.

Just so you know, standing in freezing-cold rain does not foster patience. I rang again, and when still no one came, I began banging on the door. Finally some creaky floorboards inside announced that someone was approaching.

"Hello?" a squeaky voice called out from behind the door. "What do you want?"

"It's Will Allen, Mrs. Hoffsteadtler." I replied. "I'm here to see Gerald."

The clicking and clacking sound of locks being unlatched came from the door. It creaked open a bit, but then stopped. An eye appeared in the crack.

"*Who* are you?" the voice chirped.

"Will Allen," I repeated. "I'm a classmate of Gerald's. I'm here to work on a project with him."

After a long pause in which the eye nervously scanned me up and down, the door finally opened. "Oh, all right then. Come on in."

Once I set foot inside, the door slammed violently shut and was locked before I even stepped off the mat.

"Gerald!" his mother shrieked. "Someone is here to see you."

"Coming!" Gerald's voice echoed from somewhere above. "I'll be down in just a sec!"

I don't know what it is about parents these days, but while we waited, Gerald's mother looked me over with the same disgust on her face that Rhonda's mom had. In all fairness, I *was* dripping all over her spotless hardwood floor, but still, she recoiled like I was spouting pus.

"Um, can I get you something?" she asked uncomfortably, wrapping her arms around herself as if to ward off a sudden chill. She was a tiny little person, smaller than me, and her scrunched eyes, pointy face, and bowed posture reminded me of a mouse – an overlarge mouse wearing lots of pearls and diamonds, that is.

"A towel?" I requested.

"Ah, terribly sorry," she mumbled. "All of our guest towels are in the wash. Bad timing for you, I'm afraid."

"Yes," I grumbled. "Definitely bad timing."

Like a true mouse, Gerald's mother darted her eyes, and then her head arched as if someone had called her name. She tottered off toward the stairs, where her gaze turned upward, expectantly. I took that moment to look around. From the outside, the house appeared small compared to the rest of those in that posh neighborhood, but still it was way bigger than mine. Even so, the interior felt cramped, mainly because there was so much…*stuff* filling every bit of space. The foyer was framed by a coat rack, bench, and cabinet, with every inch cluttered with jackets, knapsacks, gloves, umbrellas, purses, books, knick-knacks, papers, grocery bags, shoes, scarves…you name it. Now, to *my* mom, stuff like that is what closets are for. Or trash bins.

"Working on a project, you say?" Gerald's mother asked.

"Yes, ma'am."

"Well, you're very lucky to be working with Gerald," she said. "He's one of the brightest boys in the school, after all. I'm sure you will accomplish something great together."

"We'll do magic," I replied casually, though my fingers curled tightly like they needed to throttle something. "As long as we have the right tools."

"Oh, don't worry about that! We have anything you need: a top of the line computer, high speed internet, an art studio, a 3D printer, lab equipment…"

Just then the sound of footsteps came pounding across the ceiling in the direction of the stairwell, and Gerald appeared on the landing above us. I quietly fumed when I saw that he was still dressed in that leather jacket like the one his spoiled-brat buddies wore. At the top of the stairs, Gerald stopped to straighten his clothes and run a comb through his slickened hair. He checked himself in the mirror above the railing, and wiped some undetectable smudge from his pointy, carrot-like nose.

"Hard to believe," I muttered to myself, "that this is the same guy I had to talk into washing green slime off his head."

Gerald primped some more and pasted a big smile across his freckled, weaselly face, but then he turned and saw me in the foyer and his eyes grew wide. He recoiled, but didn't speak, so we simply stood there glowering at each other.

"Right, well," his mother said awkwardly. "I'll leave you two to work your miracles!"

And then she scampered off, leaving me and Gerald locked in a frozen stare. At just that moment, a clap of thunder struck, booming through the air around us. I shuddered from the sudden roar, but Gerald jumped like a kangaroo on an electrified floor. He almost toppled down the stairs, but caught himself, and then looked up at me again.

"What are you doing here?" Gerald finally asked.

"Didn't you engage the services of the Monster Detective Agency?" I said in a very professional voice.

"I hired Jeannine..." he started to say.

I cut him off. "But *I've* been assigned to investigate this case."

An awkward silence fell, and for a few moments the room was smothered by the muted roar of the storm that struggled to burst its way in.

"Look, if it's all the same to you," Gerald finally said. "I'll wait until the Jeannine shows up. She took care of everything last time, so I know she'll get the job done."

"You don't get it. Jeannine's not coming. She's busy."

Gerald looked away, and his head shook angrily.

"She's ditching me again, isn't she?" he hissed.

"Jeannine doesn't ditch people!" I roared.

"Well sure, says *you*. You fed me the same line last year every time she found some excuse to not show up. I guess I'm still not cool enough for her, huh?"

"I told you she's busy!"

"Yeah, right. She's busy. So then what... she gives up and sends in the 'B' team?"

The 'B' team? Did that little worm really call me the 'B' team?! My cheeks started burning, and it was all I could do to keep from spouting flames.

"It's me or no one," I growled.

Gerald twitched as he thought it over, and I'm a little ashamed to admit that I enjoyed watching him squirm.

But only a little.

"Oh, can this get any worse?" he moaned. Personally, I found his negative attitude annoying.

"That depends," I said. "Does having a monster pick its teeth with one of your ribs count as worse?"

"Great. Just great..." he grumbled, and then turned without another word and headed back toward his room. Halfway across the landing, Gerald stopped and looked back down at me.

"Well, are you coming, or are you just going to stand there dripping all over the floor?"

Steam was churning through my veins as I stormed down the hallway at the top of the stairs, but when I stepped into Gerald's room, I forgot everything else. Now, I've been in some pretty grand rooms in my time – ones lined with big screen TVs and covered with signed pictures of movie stars and ball players, but this room was like nothing I had seen before. It wasn't large or majestic: far from it, the space was cramped and the decorations were simple, plain, and worn. But just the same, for me it was like a picture of heaven.

This is my dream room, I thought.

For starters, the ceiling was painted midnight blue, with glow-in-the-dark stars pasted on them in patterns of constellations, and the walls were a mix of slate and turquoise like a placid desert sky. A powerful telescope stood by the window, and a chemistry lab was spread out across the shelf above his dresser. On his desk sat a huge mess of papers, comics, and schoolbooks, but also a big flat-screen computer monitor and globes of the earth and the night sky on either side. Next to that, his big four-post bed was covered with a 'Spaceman Bob' quilt, and topped with a blue, frilled canopy (Honestly, what *boy* has a bed with a canopy?). But the room's luster was tarnished for me when I spotted the James Dean poster that was sloppily plastered above his night stand. I gazed around at the rest of the room, which was lined with bookshelves filled with thick volumes about astronomy, spaceships, dinosaurs, and moviemaking, but also copies of *Treasure Island, 20,000 Leagues Under the Sea, The War of the Worlds*, and lots of comic books. Above some of the shelves were posters for movies including *Mission to Mars, King Kong,* and *Rebel Without a Cause*, but also faded drawings of costumed figures, dragons, astronauts, and…

"Is that Steven Hawking, the physicist?" I asked.

Gerald nodded, and I whistled in awe.

"Where did you get a Steven Hawking poster?"

"From the bookstore downtown," he said proudly. "They put it up when one of his books was re-released last year. When they took down the display, I asked if I could have it, and they gave it to me."

"Wow! You lucky dog!" I muttered admiringly.

"Don't you call me that!" Gerald fumed. "I am not a dog!"

"You…You're right," I muttered as the lids of my eyes tightened like drums. "You're no dog. In fact, you're nothing like a dog. Dogs are loyal."

"That's a laugh. Who are *you* to be talking about loyalty?"

"Excuse me," I growled, "but who stood up for you when Jacko McNulty was using you for target practice?

Who bailed you out when half the football team wanted to turn you into their tackling dummy?"

"I don't know – who?" Gerald barked back. "It sure wasn't you. Seems to me that *I* was the one who stood up for *you* when Jacko and the rest of those goons cornered us in the hallway. All *you* did was suck up to those jerks."

"I was keeping us out of trouble!"

"Yeah, right. Real brave of you. Now Jeannine, *she's* got guts. She can take on even the worst monsters. I know, I've seen her in action."

"Well, she can't have done too great a job on *your* monster, seeing as how it's back again."

"It's not the same monster, you idiot!" Gerald injected.

"...And anyway," I continued, "I've defeated lots more monsters than...wait. *What*? What do you mean it's not the same monster?"

"Do I stutter?"

"Your...your monster is a Banshee," I stammered. "I know. I read Jeannine's case file."

"That monster is gone. This one is something new. Something completely different."

My stomach churned as though the floor dropped out from beneath me like on a carnival ride. The case file had told me everything I needed to do to overcome Gerald's monster, so I hadn't been too worried about facing it even without my MonsterScope and RevealeR. But now Gerald was telling me that this was something new, something undiscovered. And my special tools were powerless to help me find it. At best, I was a blind man walking through a hamburger factory. At worst, I was one of the cows.

You have within you everything you need to defeat monsters, Bigelow had said. *Find the source, and what you seek will be there waiting for you.*

"But what is the source, Bigelow?" I mused. "And how do I find it?"

"Excuse me, but what are you mumbling about?" Gerald said. "Who is Bigelow?"

Mental note: stop thinking out loud.

"Never mind," I said. "Let's just get on with it. Why don't you start by telling me about this new monster of yours."

"What do you want to know?"

"Everything! But let's start with the basics – what does your monster look like?"

"I don't know. It mostly stays out of sight, but I do spy something moving in the shadows sometimes when the room is dark."

"Well then," I reasoned. "I guess we'll need some shadows if we're going to get a look at this thing."

And I went and turned out the light. Darkness swarmed in, and the stars pasted across Gerald's ceiling glowed softly against the midnight blue haze that flooded the room. Out of habit, I pulled out my MonsterScope and raised it to my eye.

"What's that?" Gerald asked.

"It's my MonsterScope," I answered.

"Jeannine didn't have one of those."

"Well I do. It helps me see better."

But the glass had no glow, and when I peered through the lens, everything looked exactly the same as it did without it.

"Useless," I grumbled. I shoved the scope back into my pocket, but then continued searching.

"So when you spot something in the shadows," I said as I crept slowly through the room, scanning back any forth for signs of movement, "what *exactly* is it that you see?"

"Well I...I don't know," Gerald said quietly.

"You don't know?" The hackles on the back of my neck began rising again, but I delved deeper into the thickening haze. "Can you tell me *anything* about what it looks like?"

"N-not really," Gerald stuttered. "It's always too dark." The dense fog grew heavy, and pressed on me like I was walking through molasses.

He's lying, a voice in the back of my head said.

"Hmmm. Okay," I hissed through my teeth. "Well, does it say anything?"

"No! No, nothing."

More lies!

Now like I said before, I try to be an upbeat kind of guy, but once again I was struggling to get vital information, and once again the person who wanted my help was lying to me. It was maddening.

"All right," I growled. "Let's try something else. When did this new monster first appear?"

"Um, a little over a week ago."

"Good! And did anything special happen that day?"

Gerald squirmed. "Why are you asking me all these questions?"

"Because I need to figure out what you did that caused your new monster to appear."

"Whoa!" Gerald protested. "Hold on! Jeannine didn't do stuff like this."

"Stuff like what?"

"She didn't interrogate me like I'm a crime suspect or something."

"All of these questions are important if we're going to learn the truth about your monster," I explained.

"Who cares about that? Why don't you just wave your magic flashlight around like Jeannine did and make the monster disappear?"

"My flashlight…" I hesitated. "…doesn't work that way. And since you've done this before you should already know that I can't defeat your monster without understanding it."

"I don't know what you're talking about! And I am not going to let you treat me like a criminal."

"I suppose you'd rather I treated you the way those snooty new friends of yours do?"

"Leave them out of this!" Gerald shouted. "Just do what you came here to do!"

"That *is* what I'm doing!"

"Well do it differently! Because I'm not answering any more of your stupid questions!"

"Yeah? Well if you don't want to do this my way, feel free to handle it yourself! Oh wait, you CAN'T handle this yourself - that's why you called me in!"

"Well, a fat lot of good you're doing so far!"

"I could do a lot more good if you'd help me figure out what kind of monster it is!"

"I thought," Gerald said pointedly, "that it was *your* job to do that."

That was the last straw.

"I've had enough!" I shouted, turning back to Gerald. "I'm tired of wasting my time! If you won't help, I'll…"

"Stop yelling at me!" Gerald screeched.

But at just that moment, I heard something: a hum, like the noise that floats around everywhere from bulbs, refrigerators, and all the other stuff that you never notice except when it's really quiet. Only this noise seemed to be stepping out of the background like a haunted figure emerging from the shadows, and as it did, icy tingles stung up and down my spine. Gerald stiffened too.

"Do – do you hear that?" he whispered.

The hum grew louder and surrounded us, and as it drew closer I instinctively reached for my RevealeR.

"Come on, you…" I whispered. But when I spun and pointed it around, the RevealeR remained cold and lifeless. I twitched and turned, staring deep into the void, but surrounding me was nothing. Nothing but a droning noise that pierced the silence, and a cold, hungry darkness.

Chapter 8 - Misdirections

The chill that festered in the smothering gloom gripped me tighter than the claws of a harpy. As my knees shivered, the biting hum grew into a faint roaring, like a cheering crowd at a distant football game.

"What…what's going on?" I wondered out loud. "Where is that humming sound coming from?"

"N-not a hum," said Gerald, who, like me, was suddenly shivering. "More of a…a buzzing."

"Call it whatever you want!" I shot back angrily. "But what is it and where is it coming from?"

Gerald's posture stiffened, and he twitched nervously. His head cocked from one side to the other like a rabbit scanning for predators. "How do *I* know? You're the detective, remember?"

I growled under my breath, but then continued looking around. The noise seemed to follow me through the room, and its vibrations stirred a tingling in my fingers.

"Well?" Gerald called to me impatiently.

"Something is here," I whispered. "I can feel it. A presence."

But that wasn't the only thing I was feeling. At that very moment, my insides churned from something even more stomach-turning than monsters - the indigestion I had gotten from my mother's cooking. I hadn't thought of it beforehand, but her Shepherd's Pie always makes me gassy. I kind of hoped that it would go unnoticed, but...

"What's that smell?" Gerald asked.

"I don't know," I mumbled sheepishly. "Monster breath?"

"I never *smelled* my monster before," Gerald muttered. "I just..."

"Yes?"

"Never mind!"

"Oh come on, Gerald! If you want me to help, you have to tell me what we're facing here!"

"Stop shouting at me! I told you I don't know!"

What an idiot! The voice in the back of my head cried out. *You'd think he would make more of an effort to be helpful. After all, you're trying to save him from a monster.*

"You would think that, wouldn't you?" I agreed.

"What?" Gerald grumbled. "Who are you talking to?"

He's a complete fool, isn't he?

"You got that right," I grumbled. "I mean imagine not

90

knowing who I'm…wait a second…*who AM I talking to?*"

"You are definitely losing it," Gerald muttered, turning away and shaking his head. Strangely, as he did, his trembling began to ease.

But I ignored Gerald, because I suddenly realized that the voice in the back of my head was talking to me – *out loud.*

"Gerald, do you hear it?" I whispered.

He can't hear me, spoke the voice from the darkness.

"He's here!" I called out.

"Who's here?" Gerald said.

"The monster! He's close. I hear him!"

He doesn't believe you.

"Hear him? What are you talking about?" Gerald said. "The only sound is that buzzing noise. And even that is fading."

"Seriously? Are you deaf?"

"No, I'm not deaf! Maybe you're just hearing things!"

Embarrassing, isn't it? Taunted the voice. *Perhaps he's right? Perhaps you're simply imagining this? After all, believing in monsters is only for silly children's games.*

"This is no game!" I shouted.

"Jeez," Gerald grumbled. "No wonder everyone says you're a dweeb."

You see? It's just you and me. The voice was stronger, nearer. *But playtime is over now. Are you ready to end this foolishness?*

My neck prickled like a jolt of electricity had shot up my spine. The voice, and the tingling sensation running through me, drew me toward Gerald's desk. Deep in the shadows, something stirred.

"Wait!" I whispered. "Over there!" Instinctively, I tried pointing my flashlight at what I saw, but it was still lifeless.

Meanwhile, the murky haze by the desk had grown thicker, and the glowing stars on Gerald's ceiling turned as foggy, dim, and distant as real stars. But through the thick atmosphere, something came into view: sitting in Gerald's chair was the blurry silhouette of a human-shaped form.

"Gerald! It's here! The monster!"

"Where?" Gerald whispered, squinting hard. "Where do you see it?"

Now, it was dark in Gerald's room, but it wasn't *that* dark.

"What do you mean, where?" I hissed, looking back at him. "It's right in front of you, sitting at your desk!"

"You're crazy!" Gerald said. "There's nothing there."

"Don't call me..."

At that very moment, a roar of harsh laughter shook the room, and drew my attention back to the desk. As my eyes adjusted to the darkness, the image buried in the fog sharpened. In the chair there sat a figure wearing a long, red, buccaneer-type jacket, and a three-cornered hat with a skull and crossbones insignia on the front. Waves of thick black hair flowed from the hat and down the front and back of the jacket, which ran all the way to a knee-high pair of buckled, leather boots. The monster was making muffled chomping noises, and as I stepped closer I saw that it was digging into what appeared to be a lobster dinner that was on a plate sitting on the desk.

"No wonder my mom tells me not to bring food to my room," I whispered to myself. "It really does attract pests."

I'm not sure if the monster heard that or not, but he turned and looked at me, and though his hat concealed most of his face, I could see his mustache-covered lips curl into a grotesque, evil smile. Without a word, the monster reached down to the lobster and pulled off its claw. Then he brought his other arm forward, and I gasped. The monster's arm ended in a jagged, bloody stump.

My dinner began climbing its way back up my throat, which was especially disgusting since it had been pretty nasty in the first place.

"Geez," I moaned. "And I thought that Shepherd's Pie tasted bad going *down*."

The monster smiled again, and then thrust the lobster claw into his stump. It dug in, and then snapped open and shut while drops of blood dripped from the hooked tip that poked out of the sleeve.

My stomach lurched. I pitched forward and gagged. "Oh, boy. I think I'm gonna...."

But I couldn't finish speaking, for a wave of dread washed over me. My knees started shaking like they did the time I drank a whole bottle of Gatorade in the car and then had to wait two hours before the next bathroom stop.

"What is it?" Gerald shook my arm. "I don't see anything!"

"Are you blind?" I yelled as the shaking spread to my hands. I pointed my RevealeR at the monster, but instead of giving light it grew painfully cold, like grasping a frozen rail in winter.

"Come on!" I cried, shaking it frantically. "Turn on, you piece of junk!" But nothing came out. My heart began pounding like a jackhammer.

"What's wrong with you?" Gerald spat. "Some detective you are!"

But I barely heard Gerald, because the throbbing beat of the pulse pounding through my temples drowned out everything else. It took everything in me to stifle the urge to drop my flashlight and run.

Control yourself, I thought. *Calm yourself the way Bigelow taught you.*

So in spite of my racing heart, I fought to take a deep, slow breath.

"Focus," I told myself. "Steady your breathing. Calm your body and mind."

But just then, a deep, penetrating wail startled me. The monster straightened himself and rose from the chair. He leaned his head back, and his mouth cracked open. Waves of black rain poured out that defied gravity by falling from the Earth to the sky. Echoes of dark laughter bounced off of the walls, beams, and bedposts, until it seemed that they were attacking from every direction. Out of habit, or maybe desperation, I once again pointed my lifeless RevealeR at the monster. Deep in the shadows, another laugh echoed; darker, colder, and more distant.

"Don't be ridiculous," the monster hissed. "That childish toy o' yers can't help ye now."

"Please," I whispered to my RevealeR as I held it up between me and the monster. "Please… I *need* you to help me."

Nothing happened. The monster let out another hearty laugh, and drew close. I staggered back, but stumbled into a wall, which I scratched at desperately for a way out. The dark figure rose above me, and I cowered as he raised his gleaming claw to strike.

Suddenly, my flashlight shook in my hand. Just as the monster swung his claw at me, the RevealeR sputtered, and then, like a dying man gasping his final breath, it coughed up a small drop of light that erupted outward, staining the darkness. The radiant speck, roughly the size of a dragonfly, began flying and dancing around the monster's head. He flailed his arms at the light, trying to drive it away.

"Shoo!" he shouted. "Begone, ye annoying creature!"

I breathed a sigh of relief, because I knew the monster could never win that battle.

"Ha! Chew on that," I whispered. "You can't fight light!"

Those words had barely escaped my lips when the monster swung its claw and swatted the tiny, glowing dot like a baseball, knocking it into a dark corner of the room. The light shook and flickered, but it remained where it fell and lay there quietly fading. The monster smiled broadly at the fading of the light, then he turned back to me.

"Now yer mine," he announced coldly, drawing close once more.

"No," I whispered. "Oh, no…" But there was no retreat.

I stared up into the wicked, black eyes of the monster and all I could see was emptiness. I slowly sank to my knees as doom closed in upon me.

At just that moment, Gerald appeared from out of nowhere and nudged me roughly.

"All right, enough," he said coarsely, "This is completely useless."

Then, before I could say a word, he walked over to the wall and switched on the lamp. The room lit up immediately, and when I turned back to the monster, he had vanished, along with the laughter, the humming, and everything else.

"I guess the monster isn't coming out tonight," Gerald said casually. "I knew I should have waited for Jeannine. We can try again when we have her with us. She's really good at this stuff."

I was speechless.

"Huh? What?" I said, finally emerging from my stupor.

"I really need to get started on my homework now," he intoned. "So, if you don't mind?"

"Try again?" I mumbled. "What are you saying?"

"Hit the road!" Gerald shouted.

I was too flustered to even get angry at him. I stuffed my frigid, lifeless flashlight into my pocket and left without a word.

My mind was in such a jumble when I got home that I walked right past my mother without even noticing her lying asleep on the living room couch.

"Bigelow!" I called out once I reached my room. "Bigelow Hawkins, come on out!"

The room remained deathly still, but for some soft rumbles coming from my terrarium.

"Bigelow, come on! I need *real* help this time. I almost got sliced up like Swiss Cheese tonight! You've got to give me something better than *find what you need yourself*."

But again there was no reply.

"Bigelow, stop playing your stupid head games with me!" I pleaded.

The silence held. After a few seconds wrapped in its numbing muzzle, I pulled my barren RevealeR from my pocket. Its cold gripped me.

"Bigelow?" I whispered into the bitter stillness, which absorbed my voice and gave nothing in return. I turned to my Teddy Bear, who sat looking sad and lonely on my bed. Next to him lay Bigelow's hat, quiet, empty, and still. A chill ran through me.

"I…I'm alone."

My body shivered, but then weariness stormed in as the last reserve of energy fending it off collapsed. I fell asleep before my head hit the pillow, which, as it turns out, was a bad thing to do, because my head ended up *missing* the pillow and banging hard on the bed frame instead. My brain revived just long enough to register throbbing pain, and then passed back into oblivion.

I was still in such a daze the next morning that I was standing at the bus stop for twenty minutes rubbing the bruise on my forehead before I remembered that it was Saturday, and there was no school. But what was even crazier was the fact that once I realized that, I had no idea what to do with myself. I didn't feel like going home, so I walked over to the park down the street.

"What a dump," I grumbled at the rusty swings, broken carousel, mottled ground, and dreary grey sky suspended overhead. Still, I had nowhere else to go, so I threw my book bag down next to the see-saw and plopped down onto a swing.

As I sat gazing blankly at the ground, my arms drew themselves tightly around my shoulders to fend off the icy mist that enveloped me.

"What am I going to do?" I whispered. "Where do I go from here?"

Just then, some of the haze on the eastern horizon broke, and a sliver of sunlight poured through. The rays struck my cheek, and from where they touched, warmth began to spread. I looked around, and the park came to life like a carnival that turned on the power switch. Everything that the light stroked flooded with color: the grass, trees, flowers, even the swings and monkey bars. I leaned back on my seat, which began to sway.

A little bit of rocking later, my body was soaring back and forth through the air. As the swing flew and the breeze ran through my hair, I smiled.

It's been such a long time since I've done this, I thought. *Why did I ever stop? How can I have forgotten how good it feels?*

For some reason, the whole world seemed different from the seat of that swing. As I soared through the air, I looked up at the sky as though I hadn't seen it in ages. On the eastern side of the heavens, a white rabbit cloud drifted along behind a marching band of floating cotton candy. The western horizon, however, swirled with bleak, distant tempests as far as my eyes could see. Those storms marched grimly toward me, stamping out the sunbeams as they passed across the landscape.

What I needed to do suddenly became clear.

"Will? Will Allen?" was the way a bleary-eyed Mrs. Fitsimmons answered her door. "What on Earth are you doing here?"

"Is Jeannine home, Mrs. Fitsimmons?"

"Well, of course she's home!" she growled. "It's eight o'clock on a Saturday morning! Where else would she be?"

"What is it, Will?" Jeannine said, emerging from behind her mother.

"Jeannine Fitsimmons!" her mother exclaimed. "We do not answer the door in our nightgowns!"

"I'm wearing my robe, mother!" Jeannine shot back. "It seems to me that I've seen *you* entertain guests in your robe lots of times!"

Apparently, her mother had no answer to that, so she turned back to me and complained, "And eight o'clock on a Saturday is much too early for unannounced visits. I think I shall be speaking to your parents about your serious lack of propriety!" But then she relented and let me in.

"Oh, by the way mother, your robe has a hole in it."

"A hole? Where?"

"Right above your, um, you know…"

Jeannine's mom screeched, and dashed from the room.

Jeannine smiled broadly. "Two points," she whispered gleefully. But then she turned and saw the serious expression on my face, and her smile faded.

"What?" she asked. I looked around and shook my head. Jeannine nodded, and led me to the living room. We sat silently.

"What is it, Will?" she finally asked. "Was there a problem at Gerald's house?"

I didn't look up.

"Jeannine," I whispered weakly, "I'm going to have to give Gerald's case back to you. I'm done."

Jeannine looked at me, horrified.

"Quit?" she spat. "You're going to quit?"

"No!" I said fiercely. "No, I'm not quitting! I just can't do it anymore."

"Look, Will, I know you have issues with Gerald, but that's no reason to give up on him. You kept at it even though it took a couple of tries to defeat Duncan Williams' monster, and he was much more of a louse than Gerald could ever be."

"You're not understanding me. This isn't about Gerald. I *can't* do this anymore. I think it's over for me."

"Over?" she puzzled. "What's over?"

"Being a monster detective," I said sadly. My head shook as I fought against letting the words out. "I...I can't do it anymore. You're going to have to take over from now on."

Jeannine's eyes widened, but then she took a deep breath, and her face took on the expression she wears when we're on a case: serious and firm, but also concerned and inquisitive.

"Tell me what's going on, Will. Tell me what happened. And this time, tell me everything."

So I told her everything. I told her about my RevealeR going dark, my MonsterScope turning to a dumbbell, Bigelow telling me to find the source of power, and the monster in Gerald's room.

"That monster," Jeannine said. "That *pirate*. It seems to have really gotten to you."

I nodded.

"I've never felt so helpless, Jeannine." A sudden shiver jolted my spine. "It wasn't just that my RevealeR didn't work. I was lost. So lost I couldn't even think straight."

100

"And Gerald?"

"Gerald? He was completely clueless. He had no idea what was going on," I concluded. "But the part I don't get is: why did Gerald hire us to get rid of this monster in the first place, when he doesn't even notice it when it's there?"

Now you might think that after those painful confessions, the least I could expect was a little sympathy. If you believe that, you don't know Jeannine.

"Oh, don't you see, Will?" she said in that maddeningly know-it-all tone of hers. "You've been tricked!"

Just so you know: *never* tell a detective he's been tricked. It hurts his professional pride.

"I don't know what you're talking about!" I said angrily.

"But it's so obvious!" she said. "That clawed pirate wasn't Gerald's monster. It's *yours*. Somehow, you must have brought him with you."

My mouth fell open and twitched like I was gasping for air. It's possible that a little drool dripped out, but I'm not owning up to anything. "That...That's not possible," I stuttered.

"Isn't it?" Jeannine asked impatiently. "Then why did you see it, but not Gerald? Why did it get you so scared, and yet didn't affect Gerald at all?"

My eyes squinted as though the sun had suddenly dawned. "*My* monster?" I whispered. "But, I already conquered all my monsters."

"So did Gerald. But I guess maybe monsters are like roaches. Even if you get rid of them, eventually more can show up."

"But...but how? Why?"

"I don't know," Jeannine answered. "But something has been bothering you for weeks now. Maybe this monster has something to do with it."

"I don't think so," I muttered. "It takes a powerful fear to give life to a monster, and I haven't had anything scare me like that for a long time."

"Well *something* must have rattled you."

"No, not that I can think of. Nothing much has happened lately."

Except that exploding mess in my locker incident, I thought to myself. *And I doubt that I'm dealing with a terrible ketchup monster.*

I looked at Jeannine, but decided that the incident wasn't worth mentioning.

"This was *my* monster," I mused. It made so much sense, I don't know how I didn't see it before. "Of course." Once that thought unlocked my mind, it began whirling about a mile a minute.

A new monster, I pondered. *My RevealeR going dark. Bigelow disappearing. Somehow, it all must be connected. But how?*

Find the source, Bigelow had told me. *And what you seek will be there waiting for you.*

What is it?

You must discover that for yourself.

Bigelow's words, and his disappearance, could mean only one thing: if I was going to discover the source and unlock the key to this mystery, then I had to face this monster again.

"Jeannine, I've got to go back," I said. "*Tonight.*"

Jeannine smiled broadly.

"That's the spirit," she said.

"You've got to come too," I told her.

"You want me to come with you?" she said, backing away. "But I told you I don't have time in my schedule."

"Jeannine, I *need* you to come! I don't know what this

monster is, and I have nothing to fight it off with! You understand me, you understand Gerald, and your RevealeR still works. That means you can shine light on our monsters. I can't!"

Jeannine took a deep breath and brought her hands together, then stared me straight in the eye.

"I'm your partner, Will," she said, patting my shoulder. "If you need me, I'll be there. I'll skip my rehearsal for tonight."

I smiled at her.

"Thanks, partner."

But as she removed her hand from my shoulder, she added, "But can we fit it in between seven and nine tonight? I've got dance class until six-thirty, and I'm supposed to get to sleep early because I have to rest my voice for a session with my vocal coach tomorrow morning."

"Well then," I grumbled. "We'll just have to keep the hysterical screaming to a minimum, won't we? I'll see you at seven at Gerald's house."

Chapter 9 - Reinforcements

At 7:15, I was pacing back and forth on the porch in front of Gerald's house, muttering to myself.

"Seven o'clock, she said," I growled. "Seven o'clock. Maybe Gerald was right about Jeannine ditching people…"

"Sorry I'm late," Jeannine called out sheepishly as she came running up the steps. "My mother wouldn't let me leave the house until I…"

"Never mind that," I said, glaring at her. "But what is that you're wearing?"

Jeannine froze, and gazed up and down at herself.

"You have a problem with my outfit?"

Actually, I *did*. She was wearing another one of those fancy outfits that matched what the snooty girls at school wore, right down to the pink jacket, skorts, and designer handbag. It made me want to vomit.

"Well, it's not exactly professional-looking," I grumbled.

"Oh? And I suppose you would prefer if I wore some disgusting old hat and coat like you?"

"Well, *yeah*. If your going to be a monster detective, you should look the part."

"Really? I don't remember you mentioning that when you begged me to come tonight. And I don't recall you worrying about how I was dressed when I saved your butt the last time I helped you on a case!"

I hate arguing with her when she gets all testy like that.

"Fine! Wear whatever you want. Let's just get on with it."

I turned and stepped into the entranceway, skipped ringing the bell, and went right to banging on the door. When Gerald's mother showed up, she seemed taken aback.

"Back again? And now two of you? What kind of project *is* this?"

Jeannine and I looked at each other, and then both of us turned back to the woman and spoke at the same time.

"A science experiment," I blurted.

"An art project," Jeannine sputtered out.

Mrs. Hoffsteadtler's eyebrows shot up in disbelief.

"Well, which is it?"

Jeannine and I squirmed, and exchanged an awkward glance.

"Um, that- that is…" Jeannine stuttered. "It's a…a scientific art project."

"Yeah, uh…" I added, "It's an experiment using science to make art. We're creating computerized paintings using fractals and…and clangies, and stuff like that."

Jeannine elbowed me. "Clangies?" she hissed.

But Mrs. Hoffsteadtler nodded as though that had actually meant something. "Really? Well I certainly hope you two didn't come here expecting Gerald to do all your work for you. Just because he's such a brilliant student doesn't mean you can all keep taking advantage of him."

"It's okay, ma. I'll handle this," Gerald said as he came to the door. He did a double-take when he saw that Jeannine and I were both there. It was obvious that he had not been expecting to see Jeannine, because he wasn't wearing any of his 'cool' clothes: just a beat-up NASA t-shirt and some blue jeans. Gerald quickly brushed back his hair and said, "Don't worry. These two won't be like the others. I'll make sure that they do their share of the work."

What is that all about? I wondered.

"Oh. Well then, the more the merrier, I suppose," his mother said, though her voice sounded anything but merry. Then she turned without a word and scurried off.

"Called in backup?" Gerald said to me in a nasty tone after his mother had gone. "I guess you finally realized that I was right about needing Jeannine to tackle this."

"Yes," I grumbled. "Jeannine's a specialist in dealing with hard-headed morons."

Gerald shrugged. "That explains why she's your friend."

"What would *you* know about friendship?" I growled back.

"If you two don't mind," Jeannine interrupted. "I'd like to go deal with some monsters now. Not that I'd notice much of a difference."

The sour mood that hung over us did not improve when we got to Gerald's room. When I entered, I instantly felt the same chill that came over me the night before. The air felt heavy, as though a thick, cold fog had descended. Without a word, I took my magnifying glass out of my pocket and glanced around at the gloom surrounding us. I focused on the area around Gerald's desk and chair where I had seen the monster before, but the scope didn't show anything. My head shook in frustration, but then I turned and handed the glass to Jeannine.

"Is this your MonsterScope?" Jeannine asked, looking it over.

"Yes," I said sadly. "It won't work for me, but maybe you can use it, seeing as how you don't have one of your own."

"What about your RevealeR?" she asked, and as she spoke she began walking around the room peering through the lens of the MonsterScope.

"It won't work either. See..."

I pulled my RevealeR from my pocket and flicked the switch back and forth several times. Nothing came out.

"A magnifying glass in one pocket and dead flashlight in the other?" Gerald commented. "This is what you bring to fight monsters? No wonder you need help!"

"Hah hah!" I barked as I stuffed the flashlight back into my jacket. "I could pull a chicken out of my pocket and it would still be more help than *you've* been."

"Well maybe if you spent more time looking for the monster instead of grilling me with stupid questions we'd have gotten somewhere by now."

"We'd have gotten somewhere if you'd told the truth when you answered my questions!"

"Are you calling me a liar?"

"No, *that* goes without saying. I'm calling you a pathetic, stuck up, self-important snot!"

"You dweeby little jerk!" Gerald shot back. "At least I don't pretend to be helping someone when I'm really…"

"Would you two give it a rest!" Jeannine shouted, looking up from the desk she had been examining. Gerald and I stopped talking, and glowered at each other.

"Will, I need to speak to you," Jeannine said.

"Huh? What about?"

"I need to speak to you!" she insisted, and then turned to Gerald and added, "Would you excuse us please? I need to talk to my partner…*in private!*"

And then she grabbed me by the arm and dragged me out into the hallway.

"What's with you?" she chided after shutting Gerald's door behind her.

"What's with *me*?" I hissed. "Didn't you hear him? Did you hear what he said?"

"You're behaving like a child," Jeannine said firmly. I stumbled back as if she had slapped me across the face.

"How can you take his side?" I complained.

"I'm not taking his side!" Jeannine maintained. "I'm on *your* side! I'm here because you wanted my help, remember?"

"You call this helping?"

"Yes I do!" she said fiercely. "If you want to solve the case, this is the help you need, so get a grip!"

My cheeks burned with fury, but somehow, I knew she was right, so I fumed silently.

"Now then," Jeannine said. "Let's focus on our job, shall we?"

I twitched and shook with bottled anger, but then took a deep breath, and when I finished exhaling, I nodded.

"Good! Now, since you're having such trouble solving this case, let's get back to the basics," she said. "If we're going to conquer Gerald's monster, we need to confront the source of its power, so we've got to figure out what's going on inside Gerald's head that's making all of this happen. That means that, like it or not, you've got to start understanding Gerald."

"I already understand Gerald," I hissed. "I understand that he's a self-important, swell-headed suck-up!"

Jeannine glared at me. "Maybe that's the real problem here," she said, shaking her head.

"What do you mean by that?" I asked indignantly.

"You're mad at Gerald..."

"I hate Gerald," I corrected.

"No you don't," Jeannine insisted. "You don't even know him. If you want to see real hate, just watch what happens when my mother and her second husband get in a room together."

"We're getting off the subject," I grumbled irritably.

"The point is, your feelings are affecting your work. You're angry at Gerald, so you don't want to be understanding toward him, so you can't understand his monster, so your RevealeR can't work. *That's* why it's gone dark on you."

After picking my jaw up off the ground, I thought over what she had said and countered with, "That's a brilliant theory."

Jeannine smiled.

"But it's wrong," I insisted, wiping the smile from her face. "My RevealeR stopped working *before* I took Gerald's case."

Jeannine frowned, and then scratched her head.

"You just ruined a perfectly good theory," she grumbled.

"Sorry to mess up your wonderful theory with the facts," I said sarcastically.

"Well then," Jeannine growled. "Why don't *you* come up with something?"

"Okay," I nodded, and put a finger to my lips (but I did *not* scratch my head!). "Well, for starters, we know that Gerald is hiding something. He lied or evaded all of my questions about his monster."

Jeannine nodded. "So his monster must come from something that he's feeling embarrassed or ashamed about. Something that happened to him, I wonder?"

"Or something he did?" I suggested.

Jeannine's eyes lit up. "Or, most likely," she interjected, "something he was pushed to do."

I shook my head. "What makes you think that Gerald's getting pushed to do things?"

"Are you kidding?" Jeannine said. "Haven't you seen Gerald with those friends of his? I think he'd shimmy up a barbed-wire flagpole in his underwear if they told him to."

"Now *that's* a sight I'd pay to see."

"The...point...is..." she chewed on the words and spat them out slowly, "he would probably do embarrassing or shameful things to earn their approval."

"You mean he's spineless," I said.

"What I *mean*," she hissed, glaring at me heatedly, "is that he wants really badly to fit in, and because of that he could be easily manipulated."

"Thank you, Madame Psychiatrist."

"You're welcome!"

"Just the same," I went on, "that's only one possibility."

"Maybe," Jeannine conceded. "But I'd bet my best dancing shoes that I'm on on the right track. The real question, though, is what could he have done?"

110

"Go to the source," I said, pointing at Gerald's door. "He won't tell me anything."

"I'm asking *you*," Jeannine said impatiently. "Tell me again what you saw in Gerald's room last night before your pirate showed up. If we figure out what form Gerald's monster takes, we'll get to the bottom of all this."

"Well, I didn't *see* anything," I confessed. "but..."

"What?"

"There was a noise. A humming sound. It seemed to be coming from all around. But when I saw the pirate sitting at the desk, that sound faded, and I stopped looking for it. The pirate was the only monster I saw, so I figured the noise must have come from him."

"Maybe, maybe not," Jeannine whispered. "Maybe your monster drove away Gerald's monster. Maybe that hum you heard came from *his* monster."

"That...That's good, Jeannine! Now that I think about it, that humming noise got Gerald all jumpy. If you're right, then we need to figure out what made that sound."

"And we have to figure out the source of *your* new monster too," she added. "We need to understand where that pirate came from. He appeared when you went searching for Gerald's monster, so we'll probably have to face him again."

"Ah, good point," I replied, though my eye suddenly twitched uncomfortably.

"Well, is there anything more you can tell me about him?" Jeannine asked. "Any details that you recall could be important, even if they seem small."

"I know, I know," I grumbled, and then began poking my chin. "It's just that he seemed pretty ordinary."

"Ordinary? A monster-pirate that howled like a wolf and vomited black rain that floated in the air?"

"Right. Like I said, pretty much the usual stuff, as monster-pirates go. Except maybe..."

"Yes?"

"Except for that lobster claw stuck in his arm," I said. "There was something weird about it."

Jeannine blinked like I had splashed her face with water. "The claw? *That's* what was weird?"

I nodded. "It had a strange glow around it, and was oddly shaped."

Just then, Gerald's voice blasted through the door, calling out impatiently, "Are you two ready yet?"

The sound of his voice stung like nails on a chalkboard, but I took a deep breath and nodded to Jeannine.

"I think we *are* ready," I said. "I don't think there's any more we can do out here."

"The answers," she said, nodding in agreement, "are all waiting for us in there. Let's go."

Jeannine opened Gerald's door, and together we stepped back into the room. Gerald glared at me suspiciously as we entered, then turned to Jeannine.

"I'm glad you're back," he said. "For a minute I thought you were going to dump me with this loser again."

Now I don't need to tell you that I was ready to take my MonsterScope and shove it up Gerald's... well, somewhere uncomfortable. But Jeannine was right: I was letting my feelings get the better of me, so I inhaled deeply and flexed my fingers to stifle the urge to attack. Jeannine, on the other hand, stiffened, and her eyes turned cold.

"So," Gerald grumbled. "Did you decided what to do?"

"Yes," Jeannine answered. "We've decided to leave."

I don't know whose jaw dropped lower, Gerald's or mine.

"Excuse me?" Gerald gaped.

"I don't like your attitude, Gerald," Jeannine explained. "You're being surly and uncooperative."

"That's *his* fault," he pointed his finger at me. "Will has been…"

"Don't start throwing blame around," she chided. "The simple fact is: I can't fight the monster with you behaving this way, and seeing as how you refuse to work with Will, there's no reason for us to stay."

"You - you can't do this!" Gerald pleaded. "Please! You have to help me!"

"You'll have to help yourself," Jeannine said.

"I can't!" he cried. "You don't know what it's like! You don't know what that thing does to me!"

"We don't know," I chimed in, "because you keep refusing to tell us."

Gerald looked from me to Jeannine, who stood firm, and then back to me again. His head slumped, and he surrendered.

"All right," he conceded. "I'll do whatever you say. Just – just don't go."

"You'll answer our questions?" I asked.

Gerald's head slowly, uncomfortably nodded. "What do you want to know?"

Jeannine smiled triumphantly.

"All right then," she said. "Let's get started – for real this time." And then she walked over to the wall switch and turned off the light. A midnight blue fog instantly engulfed the room, hovering in the air around us as though it had been there all the time, just waiting to show itself. Nothing else changed, except for the walls, which turned syrupy and dirty as though they had been coated with a thin layer of mud. When I probed them with my fingers, they were coarse and sticky to the touch. But there was no humming sound, or any other sign of the monster. I turned my focus back to the area around Gerald's desk again, but still nothing was there.

"Do you boys see or hear anything?" Jeannine whispered.

"No," we both replied.

"Well then, we'll need to draw the monster out. Will, try to do exactly what you were doing right before the monster appeared last time."

"I wasn't doing anything," I answered. "I was just…"

Suddenly, a realization struck me. At that very moment, a bit of the fog enveloping me evaporated.

"…I was just asking questions," I finished, and turned to Gerald, who retreated from my inquisitive stare.

114

"Gerald, tell me again: when did the monster first appear?" I asked straight away.

"A week and a half ago," Gerald answered.

"And what did you do…"

Wait, I thought. *This is where we got sidetracked last time. Don't say what you did before. We don't want to lose focus again.*

"Um, I mean is there anything else that you can remember about that day?"

"N-No, nothing," he answered quickly. "It was like any other day."

My cheeks instantly heated with anger, but I bit my lip and turned to Jeannine.

"You see?" I whispered. "Lies!"

"Back off, Captain Obvious," Jeannine whispered back. "And let the expert show you how it's done."

If there was an Olympic Event for pushing my buttons, Jeannine would earn a gold medal. Just the same, though I could feel hot lava flowing through my veins, I shrugged and stepped aside.

"All right now, let's try something else," Jeannine suggested. "Gerald, can you tell me where in the room your monster first appeared?"

Gerald hesitated, and looked around nervously. Finally, his eyes darted to the far corner of his room.

"There," he said, pointing to his nightstand. "They were over there."

"They?" Jeannine asked.

Gerald started twitching.

"Did I say *they*? I meant *it*."

"Well, which is it, Gerald? Is there more than one of them? We need to know how many we're facing."

"I - I don't know!" he shouted nervously. "Whenever the

monster appears, it's all just a big blur to me. It's like there's this huge, black fog covering everything, and I can't see what's going on."

Jeannine slowly tilted her head, but then nodded.

"I believe you, Gerald," she said.

"You *do*?" I sputtered. Gerald turned and shot me a broad, smug grin.

"I believe that you don't know what the monster looks like," she continued. "But you know exactly what it *sounds* like, don't you?"

Gerald's smile cracked, and crumpled to bits just like my mother's tuna-noodle casserole.

"What?" he stammered. "What are you talking about?"

"You hear the monster's voice, Gerald. I know you do."

"How do you know that?"

"Yes," I echoed. "How?"

Jeannine walked over to Gerald's desk and picked up Gerald's hardcover copy of *20,000 Leagues Under the Sea* from the shelf. She whistled casually for a moment, but then turned and slammed it against the wall. I shuddered from the booming tremor, but Gerald jumped like someone had lit a firecracker in his pants.

"You're sensitive to loud noises, Gerald," Jeannine explained. "I noticed it right from the start."

"I'm not *scared* of noises!"

"It's not what you fear. It's more like you're brain is wired to react strongly to sound. Your old monster took the form of a Banshee in part because loud things disturb you so much."

"But I told you – this monster is completely different!"

"Maybe, but this new one will attack the same way."

"What makes you so sure?"

"Because it *works*," Jeannine asserted. "Loud noises

116

make you tense. Your heart speeds up, your breaths become shallow – you become anxious and easier to scare, and that's what the monsters feed off of."

And with that, Jeannine struck the book against the wall again. Gerald shuddered like it was a thunderclap, and his body tensed. At that very moment, a faint humming sound arose once more and began echoing about the room. Gerald began trembling, and looked around nervously. Jeannine laid the book down on the desk and scanned the room.

"Good work, Jeannine," I told her. "You were right about how to draw it out. But I still don't see anything."

"Me neither," she said. "Let's go check out the nightstand. That's where Gerald said the monster first appeared. Maybe that's where it comes from."

We walked together to the table, but there was nothing that appeared unusual on or around it. But the humming grew louder.

"Oh, man!" I said grumpily. "If only my MonsterScope was working. If we knew what things on the table the monster touches, we'd have a clue as to what it's here for."

At that, Jeannine raised my MonsterScope, and then bent and looked down at the table through the lens. She squinted, and moved the lens closer, and then further from her eyes. She leaned back, leaned forward, swayed her head from side to side, but then finally shrugged and tossed the scope back at me. Then she began scratching her head.

"Would you stop that?" I grumbled as I placed the MonsterScope back in my pocket. "You know that head scratching is a pet peeve of mine. And it's not like it ever helps you come up with a good idea."

But at that very moment, Jeannine's eyes widened, and she reached into her fancy pink handbag. After briefly rummaging through it, she pulled out a pair of plain, black-framed glasses with a big, "A-*HA!*" and then used them to scan the nightstand.

"There!" she pointed triumphantly. "There's the little beastie!"

"What are you talking about?" I asked tersely.

"Will, do you remember when you found a RevealeR for me in your pocket?"

"Yes. It appeared when you needed one, and was decorated with daisies like it was meant for you."

"But you never found another magnifying glass. You told me to try using my reading glasses instead, since those are what I use to help me see better."

"Jeannine, look, I'm sorry that I never found you a MonsterScope of your own, but..."

"Well, it turns out that you were smarter than you thought, because my reading glasses really *are* a MonsterScope, just like your spyglass. The monsters, their tracks, and their prints all glow when I spot them with these. And that..." she pointed at something lying on the desk, "is burning bright with fear and malice. It's a monster."

"That?" I uttered as I studied the object she pointed at in disbelief. "*Seriously?* It's just a cheap bit of twine."

"It's a friendship bracelet." Gerald injected.

"A friendship bracelet?" I gawked at Gerald. "Who would ever give you that?"

Gerald scowled at me. "My *friends*, of course!"

I moved in and examined it closely. To me, it appeared to be just a few woven strands of string with red, blue, and green strands knitted together.

"It's funny. This bracelet looks a lot like the one your friend Glenda gave you, Jeannine," I pointed out.

Jeannine stiffened, and then frowned.

"No, it's the wrong colors. A lot of cliques and gangs hand these out. It shows that you're part of the group."

"It looks pretty much the same to me."

Jeannine's face twisted with a mixed expression that was hard to read.

"You got this from J.T. Anderson and his buddies, didn't you Gerald?" Jeannine asked.

Gerald nodded.

"You must have been thrilled to be given this," she said knowingly. "You've been trying to get in with that crowd for a long time."

Gerald nodded again, then his head shook, twitched, and began bouncing around like a bobblehead doll.

"So then why aren't you wearing it?" she asked.

"Stop it!" Gerald finally shouted. "Stop probing me like some frog you're dissecting! Just stop it!"

But whatever Jeannine was doing, it was working. The humming sound was growing stronger, closer, and the air grew thick with a strange odor.

"Do you smell that?" I asked, setting the bracelet back down on the nightstand and turning my gaze up into the vapor surrounding us.

Jeannine and Gerald sniffed at the air.

"Yes, I do smell something," Jeannine said softly. "But I can't put my finger on what it is."

"Not monster breath again, I hope," Gerald grumbled.

"No," I answered. "This is sort of a flowery smell."

"More of a sickly sweetness," Jeannine corrected.

The hum roared in my ears, and as it grew louder, it broke apart, so that a multitude of humming sounds surrounded us.

"We're close now," I said. "It's all coming together."

"I told you I'd figure it all out for you," Jeannine whispered cheerfully. But right then I stiffened, and my eyes glazed over. Bigelow's words suddenly sprang from the back of my mind.

Find the source, Will. You must discover it for yourself. Only then will the RevealeR's power return.

My head nodded dimly. I turned to Jeannine.

"You did good, Jeannine," I said. "You've led us to the monster. Now, I want you to do something else for me. Something important."

"What is it, Will?"

"Leave."

"What?" she sputtered. "But the monster is close now!"

"I know. It'll be all right."

"Excuse me," Gerald injected, "but do *I* have any say in this?"

"NO!" Jeannine and I both shouted.

"Will, you need me," Jeannine insisted. "You can't do this without me. That's why you asked me to come in the first place!"

"I know," I said. "But now I'm asking you to go."

"But Will…"

"Jeannine, there's a reason that Bigelow stopped appearing. He told me that I have to solve this for myself."

"But your MonsterScope and RevealeR aren't working."

"Bigelow said that I have within me everything I need to defeat this monster. But I need to discover the source of the RevealeR's power, and somehow I know that if you stay I'll never find it. You've got me pointed in the right direction. Now, whatever it is, I need to face what's coming. I need to do this on my own."

Jeannine studied me seriously, but finally nodded.

"All right, Will. I'll go."

"Are you kidding me?" Gerald shouted. "You're ditching me NOW?"

Jeannine glared at Gerald, but then fixed her eyes back on me.

"Don't worry, Gerald," she said without taking her eyes off me. "I'm leaving you in good hands. The best."

I gave her a grateful smile, but Jeannine's expression stayed grim.

"Just you be careful, Will Allen," she whispered. "And...and let me know how it all works out."

"Of course I will," I said. "And Jeannine...thanks."

Jeannine managed to coax out a weak smile, and then left the room, closing the door behind her.

Chapter 10 - Substitutions

You know, when you're in a room that is humming with unseen terrors, your weapons are powerless, and your only backup is a shivering, whiny little louse you'd just as soon feed to the monsters as save from them, it's easy to second-guess yourself a little. And as the gloom that hung above me grew darker and settled on my shoulders, doubts blossomed.

Are you nuts? I thought silently. *You just ushered out the only person who can fight whatever it is that we're facing in here! What were you thinking?*

I looked over at Gerald, whose face had '*You're out of your mind!*' written all over it. But if that was what he was showing from the neck up, the rest of him was busy shivering in synch with the hum that filled the room. The noise was a marionette string dangling in the air, its whine making my hair stand on end like the sound of a cat screeching.

"Well," I finally said. "Are you ready?"

"Are *you*?" Gerald shot back. "How can you do this when you yourself said that your RevealeR-thing isn't working?"

"Well, I can't use my usual tools, but I still have everything I need to solve this case."

"Uh huh. Which is *what*, exactly?"

"Well," I said. "I guess we'll see."

"Wonderful," Gerald grumbled. "Well, at least you have your badge. Maybe you can give the monster a ticket for unlicensed creeping."

I frowned. For a guy who was shaking with fear, Gerald somehow still managed to act like an ungrateful jerk. But I remembered what Jeannine said about my feelings getting in the way of doing my job, and so I took a deep breath again and tried to concentrate on solving the case.

"Focus," I whispered to myself. "Try to be understanding. I need to to figure out what is causing all this. But how?"

Use your brain, I thought. *You've been ignoring the obvious. Think! A humming sound, and a bit of twine. What's the connection? What would a monster want with a bracelet?*

"Gerald, why was your friendship bracelet on the nightstand?" I asked. "You never did answer Jeannine's question: why aren't you wearing it?"

123

Gerald squirmed.

"Because...because I don't feel like it, okay?"

"I just thought...I mean, after what you must have gone through to earn it..."

"Never you mind how I earned it!"

The humming suddenly became much louder. Gerald groaned, and began shaking from head to toe.

Most likely, something he was pushed to do. Jeannine had been spot on about Gerald. What had he done that was so horrifying? Whatever it was, that was the secret I needed to coax out of him in order to solve the case, I was sure of it.

"Do you hear that?" I asked as my gaze floated up toward the source of the noise. Above us, the hazy aura that filled the air grew thick and dense. "That noise is getting closer."

The sound drew my eyes to the faint, distant stars on Gerald's ceiling. They swirled, and the glow-in-the-dark planets drifted from the surface and hovered deep in the fog.

"Turn it off!" Gerald cried as he clapped his hands to his ears. "Just...just turn it off!"

"Turn *what* off, Gerald? Where is that humming sound coming from?"

"It's...not...humming..." Gerald sputtered.

"Not humming?" I whispered. "Well then what..." But then I remembered what Gerald had said the day before:

Not a hum. More of a buzzing.

Meanwhile, the luminescent orbs floating in the mist began drifting toward us, and with them, the pounding noise drew closer.

Buzzing. To Gerald it was always buzzing. Why didn't I catch on about that before?

As that realization dawned on me, the sound grew sharper and clearer, and so did my mind.

Of course! What flies through the air, makes a buzzing noise, and frightens people?

"Gerald, were you ever stung by a bee?" I called out. Gerald turned, and as he focused on me, his shaking eased.

"Well, yeah," he answered. "Back when I was a little kid."

"That's it! That must be the fear that's tormenting you."

Gerald shrugged. "I don't think so. Those little creeps may be nasty, but I learned a long time ago that if I don't bother them, they don't bother me."

Or maybe they DO bother you, and you don't want to admit it, I thought. I was getting close to the answer, but before either of us could speak another word, the buzzing grew louder still, and then from out of the fog a cluster of hazy blobs emerged. There were more than half a dozen of them, and each was huge, at least two feet long. Their bodies radiated a soft glow of yellow and black stripes, but it was difficult to make out much detail because the fog that the monsters emerged from seem to cling to them, covering each in a purplish haze.

"Gerald, I hope you're right about bees not bothering you... because *they're here!*"

"What? N-Nooooo!" Gerald squealed, and stumbled in retreat. He backed up into his bedpost, and then banged against it several times as though it would get out of his way. On the third tap, some white, loose fabric fell from the awning on top of the bed and hung in front of his face. Gerald blinked, and studied the cloth, then his eyes lit up.

"Quick, get in here!" Gerald ordered, climbing onto his bed and spreading the fabric out across the space between the bedposts in front of him.

"What is that?" I asked.

"Mosquito netting!" Gerald called back. "Just what we need!" He pulled more of the netting down around all the bedposts to create a makeshift tent. But I was frozen, my eyes transfixed on the monster bees. The only parts that appeared to be clearly visible were the huge, dark, dimpled eyes that bulged from the sides of their heads like giant black golf balls, and the sharp, glistening mandibles that snapped at me like they were pruning shears and I was an unruly hedge.

"Strange," I whispered as I cautiously approached for a better look. The closest one cocked its head and wiggled its feelers as though it was sizing me up. "These things aren't behaving at all like real bees. Real bees are solitary flyers, but these are moving together in formation like a squadron of fighter jets."

And then as if on cue, the monster at the head of the pack waved its spindly front leg as if to say, 'Come on! Fresh meat!' And they all flew right at me.

"Look out!" Gerald shouted.

I stumbled back, and quickly scoured Gerald's room for something, anything, to defend myself with. Over on Gerald's desk sat the heavy, hardcover copy of *20,000 Leagues Under the Sea* laying where Jeannine had set it down. I picked it up and held it high like a broadsword.

"Don't worry," I called back as I raised my makeshift flyswatter at the charging swarm. "I've got this under control!" Doing my best imitation of Barry Bonds, I swung the heavy hardcover in my hands and swatted away the first bee that dove in my direction. It crashed into the wall with a sickening thud, and the others held up their attack. The second bee cocked its head back and forth, and I brandished my weapon at him like a medieval knight. Or maybe a professional tennis player.

"What do you want?" I demanded. "What are you here for?"

The monster-bee tilted its head, and its eyes focused squarely on Gerald. I sidestepped to move between them.

"No," I whispered. "You have to answer to *me* first."

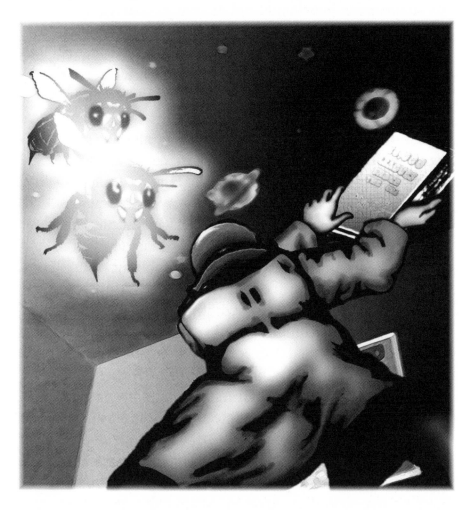

The monster gave a shrill whine, as though it was incensed at having to deal with such a rude obstruction, but then its wings buzzed faster and it dove. I swung the book as it approached, but the monster deftly swerved upward, and hovered above my head, well out of reach. All the others followed suit and lined up behind him. I stared into the multi-faceted eyes of the monster as its stinger pointed at me menacingly, and then glanced dejectedly at my now-useless weapon. Then I turned back to the hovering beast and held the copy out to him.

"Read a good book lately?"

"What are you *doing*?" Gerald shouted.

"The monsters are here for a reason, Gerald," I shouted. "If we're brave enough to face them, then we can uncover the truth and they'll weaken…"

But just as I spoke those words, the entire group suddenly circled, and then they all attacked at once. I swung my mighty book again and again, smacking and swatting in a frenzy like I was in a WWF cage match. One after another, bees splattered into the walls, desk, and door like I was shooting gigantic paintballs randomly through the room. But more kept popping up from out of nowhere, and there were so many of them that after a minute or so I was already growing fatigued. Finally, one of the bees passed through my defenses and stung me on the arm.

"Yeeeeooooow!" I screeched. I should have been thankful that the stinger didn't penetrate my jacket: instead the wound burned like the sting from a stun gun. But that blessing was hard to appreciate while staggering back in searing pain. I continued swatting away, but another bee swung around behind me and stung me in the back.

"Yaaahhh!" I bellowed. I twisted in agony, and then my legs began wobbling like an elephant balancing on a bowling ball. My vision turned blurry as I continued swinging the book blindly.

"Get in here, you idiot!" Gerald shouted.

"Don't call me an idiot, you…" But another sting, this

time on my backside, made me yelp in pain, and then jump through the netting onto the bed. I crawled on all fours like a dog while Gerald adjusted the netting around me.

"Are you okay?" he asked.

"Swell!" I grumbled.

"Then why don't you sit like a normal person?"

I tried, but when I seated myself, my butt throbbed where it had been stung, so I popped back up onto all fours.

"Being normal is greatly overrated," I decided.

"You should have come under the netting when I told you," Gerald admonished.

"And *you*," I argued, "should have told me what I needed to know about your monsters before I literally put my butt on the line for you."

"Look, I... I didn't think it would come to this! I thought you would come in here and wave your flashlight around like Jeannine did, and my troubles would be over."

"You watch too many infomercials," I commented.

"And you've been watching too many Arnold Schwarzenegger movies! What's with you, standing out there, going toe to toe with monsters?"

I shrugged.

"It's what I do," I said simply.

"It's what you do?" Gerald mumbled. "How are you still alive?"

"You know, seeing as how I've been stung so badly that I can't even sit down while defending you from monsters, the least you could do is show some gratitude."

Gerald looked down guiltily. His head shook back and forth as though he was weighing an important decision.

"Sorry. I guess you're right," he finally said, slapping me on the shoulder.

"Yeoow!" I cried. "What's wrong with you, you idiot?!"

"*What*? I'm trying to act grateful!" Gerald grumbled.

"You slapped me right on one of the stings!" I shouted.

"Oops," was his embarrassed reply.

"Enough of this," I growled. "Why don't you make yourself useful and help me fight these things?"

"Without any weapons?" Gerald scoffed. "Why don't we wait them out instead. Eventually they'll get bored and fly off."

"But I don't want them to fly off!" I insisted. "We've got to face these monsters and get to the bottom of this, here and now!"

"Excuse me, but where was all this bravery when Jacko McNulty and his gang cornered us in the hallway?"

"I was just as brave then as I am now!"

"Really? Didn't seem that way when you were busy sucking up to that clown."

"I wasn't sucking up, I was being sensible! And you goading half the football team into pummeling us wasn't bravery, it was stupidity!"

Gerald glared, but then he got a funny glint in his eye.

"Well it sure looked to *Tiffany* like it was bravery," he said smugly.

"Well it wasn't! My monster detective mentor, Bigelow Hawkins, taught me that even after you conquer fear, there are still lots of other feelings that make you do stupid things. And that was one of the stupidest…"

At just that moment, a sound caught my ear. The background noise of buzzing had become staticky and intermittent. I turned and spotted the bees, hovering patiently just outside the netting. They were all gathered directly in front of Gerald – now that I wasn't between them and him they had completely lost interest in me – and their faces leaned toward him eagerly like puppies

130

waiting for him to come out and toss them a bone, preferably one of his own. The pitch of their collective buzz began to rise and fall as though something was modulating it. Then things turned really strange: the buzz began forming *words*.

"Stuuuppiddd…" it hissed.

Gerald's face blanched, and he gave me a sideways glance.

"Stuuuppiddd…thiiiingssss…" the buzzing said. The bees then floated closer to the netting, and Gerald's eyes widened into a plea for help.

"Well," I said mockingly, "So much for the *'wait for them to get bored and fly off'* plan."

"All right, fine!" Gerald conceded. "What should I do?"

"You have to go out there," I told him. "You have to face them."

"What? Are you crazy? You saw what they did to you! They'll sting me to death!"

"I don't think so," I said as I watched the glowing bugs flex their huge mandibles and flail their proboscises. "They seem to be trying to…*talk* to you."

And even as I spoke, the buzzing gave way to a sort of murmuring, like a hundred voices whispering at once. I reached and grabbed a corner of the netting.

"What are you doing?" Gerald wailed, sounding panic stricken.

"We need to hear what they're saying," I insisted, and then pulled back one side of our protective cocoon.

"No, don't…" Gerald pleaded much too late, jumping up to grab the netting at the last moment. Instead, he accidentally slid off the bed and found himself face to face with the bees. But they didn't attack him. Not with their stingers, anyway.

"Yooouuuu…" the monster bees buzzed in unison.

131

Unlike most kids confronted by their monsters, Gerald said nothing. He didn't shake, flinch, or cry either. He just stood there.

"Yooouu…noooo…" they echoed together.

"Yoooouu…noooo….g-goooood..."

Then the tight formation that the bees flew in broke apart, and they swarmed around Gerald, each with its own verbal sting.

"Yooou… noooo… cooool..." said one.

"Yooou…nooooo… smaaarrt..." added another.

"Yooou… weeeeak…" admonished a third. Pretty soon, the epithets were coming so fast and furious that it was almost impossible to hear each one.

"Yooou… faaaake..."

"Noooo… liiiike… yoooouu..."

Gerald was as stony as a statue, absorbing it all with a blank expression on his face, while I growled in frustration, powerless to help. I reached into my pocket and pulled out my RevealeR, but when I flicked the switch back and forth, it was still lifeless. Meanwhile, the swarm of bees closed in on Gerald.

"Come on!" I grumbled helplessly. "I need to do something. But what?"

You have within you everything you need to defeat monsters, I heard Bigelow's voice say. But what did I need? The buzzing was filling my brain, making it hard to think straight. I took a deep breath and held it, then closed my eyes.

You have within you everything you need.

"Use what's within you," I whispered to myself. "Use your wits. I can solve this. I've already seen lots of clues."

Clues like the friendship bracelet Jeannine had discovered. It should have been a prized possession, yet

132

Gerald would not put it on. But why? And what did that have to do with bees?

Bees, I thought. *Mindless creatures that have painful stings. They live only to serve their queen. And they work together in large groups like a hive, a swarm, or...*

"Or a *gang*," I mumbled to myself. "Of course!"

And I opened my eyes. In front of me, the bees were still swarming and cursing Gerald, but the fog clinging to them began to dissolve. And what I saw through the fading mists was pretty bizarre, even for monsters. Their bodies were made up of three mismatched segments. For some reason, the oblong, yellow and black striped abdomens caught my attention first. Just a thought: it might have had something to do with the dagger-like, serrated stingers jutting from the base of each of them. Every monster also had a leather jacket covered mid-section connecting its abdomen to its head, wings, and six spindly, telescoping legs. And the heads themselves were... well, plain *weird*. They were each the shape and color of a roasted almond, with huge compound eyes jutting from the top (mental note: I will *never* call my mom bug-eyed again) and crowned by a pair of curved, segmented antennae. At the other end, a long proboscis hung from jaws framed by sharp, pincer-like mandibles. But what made them weird was the fact that in between those bee-like features, the middle of each head was oddly...*human* shaped, with a nose, cheeks, and ears. It was like they were built from a crazy, insect version of Mr. Potato Head.

Those strange creatures continued circling, stinging Gerald with their verbal taunts, but now their voices were sharper, and more human.

"You're ssssuch a geek..." one monster cried.

"You are a losssssser..." another voice called out.

133

"Nobody likessss you..." said a third.

"I see you now," I called to the monsters as I climbed out onto the floor. "I know who you are!"

But the bees ignored me, all but one. It broke off from the group circling around Gerald and slowly approached.

"Ohhhhh, you think ssssssooo?" the bug-eyed creature hissed. "You knoooow me?"

As the monster hovered closer, it's head titled back and forth as though it was studying me, and I was mesmerized by a thousand images of my own face that reflected back from the facets of its huge eyes. Below those, a series of tiny dark dots covered the monster's rosy, human-like cheeks, which surrounded a pointy, reddened nose. Something about those features seemed familiar.

"That...that face..." I gasped. "It looks like..."

I turned to Gerald, who was still staring, open mouthed, at the swarming creatures. Dark freckles were splashed across his cheeks and sunburned nose.

"Gerald! It's *you*! This bee is you!"

"Yes, it's me," Gerald agreed with sad resignation in his voice.

"But...but why? Why is your face on one of the monsters?"

Gerald didn't answer. I turned to the bees and studied them from one to the other. Except for the Gerald-like details on his face, the monster in front of me looked identical to all the others, right down to the matching leather jacket. Then I looked back at Gerald. The horror in his eyes as he fixed them on the gang of monster-bees reminded me of the expression that was on Rhonda's face when she viewed her own distorted reflection in the monster mirror.

"Your fear is that this is who you are," I whispered.

"You're scared that you're the same as them."

At that very moment, my vision grew clearer, and then my RevealeR began to vibrate. It grew warm in my hand, but no light came out. It's special power was still missing.

"I guess you can't show him the truth," I said to my flashlight. "So I'll have to find a way to do it myself."

"Gerald," I called out. "This monster - he's not what he appears to be. He's not you!"

"He is," Gerald said mournfully. "Just look at him."

"He's not!" I insisted. "Monsters take the form they know will scare you. That face is what the monster knows you're afraid of. That's why it looks like you're one of them. But you're not!"

For some reason, those words finally attracted the monsters' attention. They stopped circling Gerald, and their bodies turned as one to face me. Gerald's head twitched, and then he stared at me as if he had never seen me before.

"I *am*," he said. "I am one of them. I dress like them. I act like them. I do whatever they want."

Something he was pushed to do, Jeannine had said.

"Do whatever they want? What do these monsters make you do?"

But the monsters did not wait for Gerald to answer. They floated toward me, and then one of the voices, colder and deeper than the others, called out, "Ssssstop himmmm. Desssstroy…"

In response, the Gerald-bee shuddered, then rose high into the air and dove at me. I grabbed the first thing I could reach, which turned out to be Gerald's pillow, and quickly thrust it between me and the hurtling monster.

"Oh no you don't!" I shouted as the monster crashed into my fluffy shield.

In case you were wondering, a pillow makes for very poor armor. The monster's stinger tore right through the fabric and filling, coming within inches of giving me an unplanned nose piercing, but then it got stuck in the stuffing. The bee twisted and darted about in an attempt to free itself. Feathers flew everywhere as I held on for dear life, trying to keep the monster from getting free for another try. Unfortunately, the monster squirmed loose, shredding what was left of the pillow in the process.

"Uh oh…" I whispered as I examined the tattered scraps of cloth in my hands. I stood helpless, with no defense within reach, as the monster dove at me again, its stinger aimed directly at my face.

Chapter 11 - Battle Cries

For those who haven't experienced having a flying dagger swoop at your head, let me tell you that one of the most important things to do is avoid panicking. If you lose your head while battling monsters you might just...well, *lose your head*. On its first pass, I deftly dodged the bee's stinger, and when the monster rose and flew at me a second time, I dove aside toward the desk. If the other monster-bees had joined in I probably would have been cornered, but they seemed to prefer watching the show. Some of them even cheered like they were at a ball game.

"Ouuuuuww! Nice mooove!"

"Beat him with your wings!"

"Skewer him good!"

"What a stinger!"

"Oh yeah? Well mine is bigger!"

"Hey!" I cried out. "No fair! Isn't anyone cheering for *me*?"

"*NO!*" the monsters all shouted at once.

"Not a chance!"

"You're not one of us!"

A small point, but in any match it's always better to be the home team. The Gerald-bee thrust at me again, and I fended off the stinger with the end of my RevealeR like one of the Three Musketeers. I tried to plan a counter-attack, but before I could come up with anything I tripped over Gerald's chair and tumbled to the ground. I spun, but found the Gerald-bee right above me, diving its stinger toward my gut.

"This is gonna hurt…" I whispered.

Just as I was about to be fitted with a second belly button, there was a loud THWACK, and the bee went crashing into the wall. I looked up, and there was Gerald with a thick hardcover book in his hands.

"Um, thanks," I mumbled. Gerald simply nodded. The bees, on the other hand, became frenzied.

"Foul!" cried one of them. "No helping!"

"Interference!" another buzzed. "Penalty!" In unison the swarm floated higher, and then zoomed straight at us.

Gerald and I looked at each other, and then without a word we both jumped onto the bed and pulled down the netting. The bees dove right into the netting, ripping and tearing at it.

"You have to face them... great plan!" Gerald grumbled.

"Well if you weren't trying so hard to be just like those creeps, we wouldn't be in this mess in the first place!"

"Well, excuse me for trying to fit in!" Gerald shouted. "I don't want to be treated like I'm some eggheaded geek all my life! I'm not *you!*"

My mouth dropped open, but no sound came out. Instead, the words I'd said to Bigelow just days ago rang in my ears.

If I could show people what I've faced, I had told him. *I'd be a hero, instead of being treated like some undersized, underage dweeb all the time. Don't I deserve that?*

"Maybe… maybe me and Gerald aren't so different after all," I realized. Just as the thought came into my mind, the last bits of the fog enveloping us blew away. I looked around, and even through the mosquito netting I could see everything in the room almost as clearly as if I was using my MonsterScope. To my newly keen eyes, details that I hadn't noticed before jumped out at me. The worn telescope by the window was thick with dust from lack of use. The clutter of papers on the desk had a pattern to it, like there was some unseen organization to the mess. But what stood out the most was the neatness and care with which Gerald's drawings had been framed and mounted to the wall, which contrasted strongly with the wrinkled crookedness with which some of his posters had been hung. And poking out from under his James Dean poster, I noticed the outline of several pictures beneath it that had been covered over.

There was so much more to take in, but right then the thrust of one of the bees into the netting sent its stinger directly at my nose, and that returned my attention to more immediate concerns. I thought hard and fast.

"Gerald!" I shouted. "I've got a plan!"

"Great!" he replied. "What is it?"

"Come over here," I ordered. "We need to both be on the narrow end of the bed together."

"But that end is starting to tear."

"Exactly! I'm going to draw the monsters in close."

"And me?"

"You're the bait."

Gerald suddenly doubled over in a fit of coughing.

"Um, I'm not really crazy about this plan," he wheezed.

"Just do it, you big wuss!"

"You know," Gerald growled. "You need to work on your people skills."

But Gerald did as he was told. We sat at the very end of the bed, so close to the netting that the bees' stingers were only inches away as they pressed through the cloth.

"You call this a plan?"

"Just hold still," I coaxed.

"But the bees are almost through!"

"Steady…" I whispered. "They're almost all in place…"

Then, in a flash, I jumped up and pulled the netting from the bed and threw it over the back of the swarm, then wrapped them up around and around in the cloth. They buzzed and squirmed, but were completely immobilized.

"Stop fluttering, Sally!" one bee said to another. "You're getting me all tangled up!"

I turned to Gerald and said, "Sally? You have a horrible monster named *Sally*?"

"Trust me," Gerald replied. "The *real* Sally is even worse."

"Don't tell me what to do, Darryl!" cried Sally the bee. "Now get off of me, you brainless, freckle-faced, bug-eyed blockhead!"

"I do NOT have freckles!" the bee named Darryl

140

shouted back. The two of them continued squirming and buzzing angrily, and the other bees were just as irritable.

"Get off!" one yelled. "You're all over me!"

"Be careful with that stinger!" cried another. Soon, all of them were yelling at each other.

"Stop banging into me, you potbellied pollen-sucker!"

"Hey! Watch where you're sticking your proboscis!"

"Move your antenna! It's poking me in the eye!"

"Which one?"

"Which one what? Which antenna, or which eye?"

"Get off! You're creasing my wings!"

As the monster bees grumbled and wriggled, I tied the ends of the cloth together, locking them in a cocoon of netting. Gerald gaped in amazement.

"Good work!" he cheered.

"Thanks!" I said smugly. "It was easy as…"

But before I could finish gloating, I suddenly reeled from a horrible, stabbing pain in my shoulder.

"Yeeearrgh!" I screamed. Another agonizing sting struck me on my leg, and I collapsed to the floor. When I rolled onto my back, I saw a gigantic monster bee, at least twice as large as the others, hovering above me with its stinger looking like a barbed-wire poker ready to strike once more. The human portion of the monster's face had a thin, square nose, a polka-dot bow tie around its neck, and a bad case of acne all over its bright red forehead. Thick, horn-rimmed glasses covered its insect eyes, and a beaten up Fedora hat topped a smooth mane of golden hair that fell between its antennae.

"I'm being lorded over by a circus clown with wings?" I grumbled.

The scene might have been comical, but for the fact that the monster's enormous stinger was poised to eviscerate me. And there was nothing humorous about the way its face twisted into a wide, evil grin as it drew closer. I tried to spin away, or get up, or defend myself in any way, but my arms and legs refused to respond.

"Um… *Help*?" I pleaded. But Gerald was frozen in terror, and all that came from him was a soft whimpering sound.

"I've got you noooooww," the monster hissed as it slowly descended. Its voice was a shuddering rumble as deep and forceful as the ocean. I gasped.

At that moment, the door burst open and a beam of light caught the monster full in the face, driving it back, screaming. The wielder of the light ran over to me.

"Are you all right?" she said, trying to help me up.

"Jeannine?!" I said as I stumbled to my feet. "What are you doing here?"

"Never mind that now," she insisted. "We have to finish off the monster! We have to do it now, before it can make any more bees."

Gerald shook off his stupor and gaped at her.

"The bees *are* the monsters," he sputtered.

"They *are* monsters," Jeannine said, "But they're not **the** monster. They're not your Hidden Beast."

"My what?"

"The monster behind it all," she explained impatiently. "The one that set loose all the other monsters."

"I don't know what you're talking about!" he complained.

"That's because you didn't understand what I showed you earlier," she explained. "When I used my glasses as a MonsterScope, they led me to the source of the monsters. And it was right on your nightstand."

"You mean…" I whispered.

"YES!" Jeannine announced. "The true monster is the *bracelet*!"

"The bracelet?" I said. "Seriously?"

"Serious as Mrs. McCallister's bad breath! You have to ignore the bees! You need to focus on the bracelet!"

"Are you crazy?" Gerald shouted. "If we ignore the bees they'll sting us to death! Bracelets aren't dangerous."

"Oh really?" Jeannine said in that haughty tone of hers. "Look again!"

And she shined her flashlight on the table. Sure enough, there was the bracelet, which glowed eerily in the beam from Jeannine's RevealeR. But light wasn't all that was radiating from the glistening band: it was also sprouting buds that grew into new bees at an alarming rate.

"You see? That's where they're all coming from," she told us. "That's the monster we need to deal with."

"But why?" I asked. "Why would Gerald's monster be a bracelet? Why is that frightening?"

Even as I spoke, my eyes were drawn to Jeannine's wrist. Wrapped around it was the friendship bracelet she had received from her friend, Glenda.

"It's not just the bracelet," I realized, turning to Gerald. "It's *who you become* when you wear it. You start dressing like them. You start acting like them. Then when you look at yourself, you're not *you* anymore. You're one of them."

Jeannine suddenly shivered. "That-that's good detective work, Will," she said. But her expression turned dour.

"I hate to interrupt," Gerald said crossly. "But how exactly do we fight a bracelet?"

"With the light of truth," I answered. "If we understand the monster, the RevealeR should be able to do its thing." I turned back to Jeannine, and she nodded, and pointed the beam from her RevealeR directly onto the bracelet. The bubbly, multi-colored light lit the monster like a thousand lava-lamps, but the woven band did not shrink, or change, or stop producing new monsters.

"Something wrong?" Gerald asked. "Why isn't it working?" A puzzled expression came over Jeannine's face, but then she turned and held out her RevealeR to Gerald.

"You have to take hold, Gerald," she said. "I can only show you so much. It has to be *your* truth that defeats the monster."

Gerald reached toward Jeannine, but just then one of the bees tore through the netting and worked its way free.

"Look out!" Gerald shouted, but before Jeannine could react, the monster flew at her and stung her on the hand, making her drop the flashlight.

"Oh! Oh no!" she cried as it rolled out of reach under the desk. The bee flew in front of Jeannine, backing her away from the desk. Meanwhile, more monsters continued sprouting from the bracelet. And now we were defenseless.

"Goooood work, Darryl," echoed the cold, deep voice of the super-sized monster bee as it floated back out of the shadows. "Now, freeeeee our brotherssss and ssssisterssss."

Darryl and the newly formed bees flew to the netting and began tearing at it. In moments, the rest of the monster bees sprang loose and circled above us. What made the situation even worse was that we no longer had netting or anything else to shield ourselves with. I furiously spun around seeking any weapon or means of escape.

"Jeannine, Gerald, quick!" I shouted. "Get under the bed! The bees are too big to follow us!"

We dove under, and as I predicted, the bees couldn't fit. They banged and bounced against the lower railing trying to fly in after us, but then finally hovered around the side of the bed awaiting further instructions as the three of us lay prone on the floor.

"Leave them!" their master's voice instructed. "Where can they go?"

"Well, got any new plans?" Gerald asked.

"Not unless you count screaming and running from the room in terror," I said.

"We could wait them out until morning," Jeannine suggested. "Monsters vanish at daybreak."

Gerald shook his head. "We haven't had much luck with that 'waiting them out' stuff."

"That's for sure," I agreed. "And anyway, if it's a choice between facing these monsters now or facing my mom in the morning after missing my curfew tonight, I'll take the monsters, hands down."

Gerald and Jeannine nodded in agreement. After all, they have moms too. Meanwhile the bees, unable to reach us through the narrow opening between the bed and floor, buzzed frustratedly, and seemed to lose focus.

"Sally, stop shoving!"

"Don't tell me what to do, Darryl!" Sally snarled back at him. After she pushed him aside, she used her feelers as a comb to smooth the bleached-blond braids that had become tangled with her pearl-drop earrings. "I haven't forgotten how you poked at me when we were stuck in that netting!"

"We were trapped!" Darryl protested. "I couldn't move!"

"Oh, you were just looking for an excuse to do that!"

"Was not!"

"Enough!" the giant bee commanded. Strangely, its voice turned deeper, and yet more human-sounding. "Cease your petty squabbles!"

The arguing died down, until the only sound remaining was the buzzing that echoed throughout the room.

"That's better," the cold voice said. "Now go get me what I want. You know where to find it." I spun on the floor, looking for some way that the bees might come in after us, but instead of attacking, they all flew from the side of the bed and gathered by the desk. I leaned close enough to the end of the bed to see one bee open Gerald's desk drawer and pull out two small, rectangular objects.

"Light me!" the giant bee ordered. Another bee lifted one of the objects toward the center of the pack. There was a clicking sound, and a tiny puff of flame erupted.

"What's going on?" Gerald asked. "I can't see a thing!"

"They're…they're…" I mumbled. As the circle of bees rotated, I saw…

"They're *smoking*!" I announced. "The bees are smoking cigarettes!"

"What a disgusting habit," Jeannine declared. I frowned. We both turned to Gerald, who recoiled.

"Gerald, why are your monsters smoking?" Jeannine asked.

"I - I don't know," he stuttered.

"Oh, come now, Gerald!" the voice called to us. "You know that's not true!"

"Gerald," I said. "They took the lighter and pack of cigarettes out of *your* drawer!"

Gerald looked around nervously.

"Where did you get the cigarettes from, Gerald?" Jeannine challenged. "Did you steal them?"

"No!" Gerald shouted. "I paid for them!"

"Paid for them?" I asked. "How? You're not old enough to buy cigarettes."

"Look, is that really important right now?"

"Thanks, Gerald!" called the voice. "These are first-class smokes!"

"Who *is* that?" Gerald asked pointedly. As if in answer to his question, the circle parted to reveal in its center the super-sized bee, sitting casually, and yet commandingly, on Gerald's desk.

"It's the one that all the other bees serve," I surmised. "It's the queen bee."

"I am the *King* Bee," the monster corrected. "You shall call me Apis Rex, for I am your master!"

Gerald and I looked at each other and snickered.

"There's no such thing!" Gerald commented.

"Doesn't know much about nature, does he?" I said. "That is one dumb monster!"

"Pathetic worm!" the monster replied, its ocean-deep voice suddenly turning shrill. "You think you're so smart? And yet here I sit, lording over everyone while you lay cowering under the bed like a frightened mouse!"

From my vantage point, I saw the other bees, like well-trained dogs, all nod in unison. The King Bee grinned.

"Besides," he taunted, "I always have the smarts I need whenever I want them. Your geeky friend will help me with all that *figuring things out* stuff. He always does."

My blood suddenly burned. In that instant, it all came together: the tone of contempt; the smug, self-important attitude; the wave of blonde hair. I realized exactly who the King Bee really was.

"It figures," I whispered. "I always thought he was a clown." And right then I knew what had to be done.

"Gerald," I said. "Are you ready to keep your word and do whatever we tell you?"

"Y-Yes," he said weakly.

"Well, this is your moment," I told him. "Go out there and challenge Apis Rex. It's time to conquer the King Bee and save the day."

"Conquer the King Bee? *Me?*" Gerald protested. "Why me?"

"Because you're the only one who can."

Gerald looked from me to Jeannine, who nodded in agreement. "It has to be you, Gerald. You have to face him."

"How? With what?"

"Get my RevealeR," Jeannine said. "The light of truth will give you the power to defeat him – and save us all."

"Fools!" the King Bee shouted. "You would rely on the weakest among you to fight me?"

"Hey Rexie, BUTT OUT," I called back (Yes, I gave the monster a nickname – I do stuff like that). "This is a private conversation going on down here!"

"Ha! You are all doomed!" the monster crowed. I was about to answer with one of my patented witty comebacks, but Gerald grabbed my shoulder. His eyes were wide with terror, but his face scrunched like he had something sour in his mouth.

"I don't know about you," he said firmly, "but I refuse to be cowed by a scientifically illiterate monster."

And with that, Gerald slid out from under the bed to face his monsters at last. The air grew thick as the buzzing noise and smoky fog, like a blanket of doom, closed in around him.

Chapter 12 - Confrontations

"Ah, Gerald. Good!" King Rexie said. "Now that you are here, you shall take your place, slave."

The other bees, lacking any instructions from their master, circled vacantly as Gerald made a mad dash for the flashlight, which lay under the desk.

"Stop him," the King Bee bellowed. The swarm moved to block Gerald's path. They encircled him, and hovered low in front of the desk. Gerald looked around nervously, but then turned to the King Bee and defiantly chanted, "I'm not afraid of you." I grimaced when he said that.

"That line never works," I moaned. Meanwhile, the circle of bees closed in on Gerald.

"Leave him to me!" King Rexie commanded, and the others backed away. The king then arose from his perch and floated toward Gerald until they were nose to…well, mandible. Gerald held steady, though his knees shook violently. Rexie reared back and let out a cackling roar that reminded me of the sound my mom's blender made when one of the gears broke. His face split open to reveal rows of spiked, shark-like teeth. A series of tongues waved and hissed like snakes, and then a fountain of fetid slime shot out at Gerald, who screamed and dodged.

"See?" I said smugly. "It never works."

"You are *not* helping," Jeannine pointed out irritably. "Say something useful, why don't you!"

So I thought of something.

"Gerald," I called out. "Gerald, it's okay to be afraid."

"Thanks," Gerald shouted sarcastically as he stumbled back. "I'm glad you approve."

"Be brave, Gerald," Jeannine told him. "Stand up to him!"

"I… I can't!" Gerald protested. "I'm not like *you*. I'm not strong enough!"

"Of course you can't," King Rex injected. "You are a weak, lowly slave."

"That's a lie, Gerald!" I shouted. "Get the RevealeR! Its light will show you the truth!"

"Ha! The only truth here is *my* truth," the King Bee cackled. "And my truth is that you live to be my servant. My truth is that you are a nothing but a nameless, faceless bug who does whatever I command. That's what *you* know to be the truth too, isn't it Gerald?"

Gerald wavered. When he finally glanced back at the King Bee, he lowered his eyes. "It…It's true…"

"Then stop resisting. Take your place with us."

"Gerald, no!" I shouted. But Gerald shook off my words, and then nodded to the bees. He stepped into the circle and bowed his head. The King Bee gave a guttural chuckle, and the others closed in and began probing Gerald with their feelers. Several patted him on the back.

"Welcome to the team!" said Darryl, holding up one of his spindly legs. "Give me a high-five…er, high *one*."

Gerald unenthusiastically complied, and the others cheered.

"Hey, me too!" shouted Sally.

"What's happening?" Jeannine cried. "I can't see what's going on!"

"He… He's giving up!" I sputtered. "He's *joining* them!"

Jeannine shook her head and grumbled, "Well, so much for being home by nine o'clock."

The bees circled Gerald, and began…well, *decorating* him. One fussed over his hair, while another fitted him with a leather jacket. Others were busy pasting feelers onto his forehead and fitting a stinger onto his…um, tailbone.

"They're giving him a makeover!" I said. "His hair. His clothes. They're turning him into one of them!"

Jeannine shuddered, and brought her hands to her face.

"No," she whimpered. "It's not right. That's not how real friends should treat you." She sobbed a bit, but then turned and stared at her wrist. Finally, she lowered her hands and took a deep breath.

"We've got to do something," she said resolutely, and crawled to the edge of the bed. "He needs help."

I grabbed her arm and pulled her back. "What he needs," I told her as I crawled past, "is a friend. A *real* friend."

Jeannine hesitated, but then nodded and let me pass.

"Just remember," she said. "I'll have your back."

"I know. Now, if I distract the bees enough, go for the RevealeR. Otherwise stay here where they can't reach you."

"No promises," she said. "Now go."

I jumped out from under the bed. The bees remained focused on primping Gerald and paid me no mind, but they still blocked the way to the desk and the RevealeR. I scanned around for another option, and spotted the thick hardcover book I had used as a weapon earlier. I crept toward it, and not a single bee made a move to stop me.

"I'm here, Gerald!" I shouted as I grabbed the book. I then crouched, facing the swarm surrounding Gerald while brandishing my improvised flyswatter like a sword. "I'll get you out of this!"

"Why?" Gerald looked at me and buzzed in confusion. His voice began to turn bee-like. "Why would you dooooo that?"

I took a deep breath. To be honest, when I started speaking I wasn't sure what I was going to say.

"There was a time, not long ago," I recalled, "that I stood up for you and you stood up for me. We were friends then."

"We are his friendsssss now," the bees called out as one. "We are many, you are one. We are popular, you are an outcassst."

Gerald turned his monster-decorated head from me to the monsters, and then back again. "They're riiiight. Why should I be friendsssss with you insssstead of them? Why would I choooose yooooou?"

I can't tell how much those words stung – only that they hurt worse than all of the bee stings put together. But I stayed focused and resolute.

153

"I'm not asking you to choose me," I answered. "I'm asking which Gerald do you want to be: the one you are with *them*, or the one you were when we stood together in that school hallway, shoulder to shoulder against a bunch of bullying football players? You stood up to those brutes that day. You were a hero."

"Enough," King Rexie called out. "He is not one of us, Gerald. You must sting him. You must give him pain."

At that moment, I realized why the bees had not attacked when I came out from under the bed. They wanted Gerald to do it. Gerald began moving toward me, but then hesitated.

"He... he's my friend..."

"Really?" the king scoffed. "Do you think he would still be your friend if he knew the truth about you? Or would he abandon you?"

"Don't listen to him Gerald! I'm not going anywhere!"

But Gerald shook his head sadly. His stuck-on antennae waved through the air and poked the Sally-monster.

"Hey, watch it!" she yelled, then turned to Darryl. "I told you those antennae were too long!"

"They are not!" Darryl said. "Gerald, your antennae look great on you. Tell her!" But Gerald payed no attention to either of them.

"You only defend meeee because you don't know the truuuuth," he said. "You don't know what I've doooone."

"It doesn't matter what you've done!" I said. "What matters now is what you're *going* to do! You have a choice, Gerald! Starting right this moment, who are you going to be?"

"I...I..." Gerald sputtered. "I don't knooooow."

My heart sank deep into my stomach. In spite of all he had done to anger me, I felt sorry for him.

"I wish I could help you see your true self," I said, waving my powerless flashlight frustratedly, "but my RevealeR can't show you..." Then I stopped. All around the room, the posters, globes, and other decorations called to me.

See me, they whispered.

Their images shone through the murky air almost as clearly as if they were illuminated by the light of truth.

My dream room, I recalled. *But Gerald put all this together. It's his dream too!*

"Gerald!" I shouted. "I can't show you who you are with my RevealeR. But look around! Who chose all of the posters in this room?"

"I...I did," he answered meekly.

"The books, the globes, the stars on the ceiling, whose are those?'

"Mine," he said more firmly.

"*This* is you. This is the true Gerald all around us! Look around – scientists, superheroes: people that are brave and noble! These are the heroes you've chosen. This is you. What you know, what you think, what you wish for, these are the things you are. These are the things you dream of being. And they're all around you here. Look at them!"

Gerald's head waved around as if in a daze. He glanced at the dazzling posters of scientists and costumed heroes as though he hadn't seen them in years, and then looked at himself, at the bee-like fittings all over him. His hands ran up and down the smooth leather of the jacket the bees had placed on him, and then he looked up at the newer posters sloppily plastered above his nightstand. Gerald rocked and twitched, and then he exhaled loudly. Finally, he approached, with his newly grafted stinger poised to stab me.

"Gerald...?" I took a breath and steeled myself.

In one motion, Gerald suddenly grabbed his James Dean poster and ripped it from the wall. He took the pieces in his hands and crumpled them up, muttering, "I never liked that stupid poster."

The bees instantly roared their disapproval.

"Hey, I love that poster!" Darryl cried out. "It was the coolest poster ever!"

"Well, you're finally right about something, Darryl!" Sally agreed.

Gerald tore the leather jacket from his back and brushed the antennae from his head, then spun around trying to remove the stinger pasted to his tailbone. The bees, on the other hand, kept trying to reattach everything.

"NO! Leave me be! I'm not one of you!"

"Fool!" bellowed the King Bee. "You reject us? You choose to be an outcast? Then you have chosen PAIN!"

And with that, he waved his leg, and the bees stopped trying to make Gerald one of them. Instead, they began stinging him with their stingers. And every sting came with an insult.

"Loser!" (*Sting*)

"Dweeb!" (*Sting*)

Gerald writhed in agony. I jumped in and began swatting them away, but newly formed bees kept adding to their ranks, and I was ridiculously outnumbered.

"Gerald, I can't keep this up for long! Go get the RevealeR! It's what you need to defeat the monsters!"

Gerald arose and tried to fight his way to the desk, but his path was blocked.

"Oh no you don't," said Sally as she hovered in front of him. "No toys for you, you traitor!"

I struggled to clear a path to the desk for Gerald by lunging forward and swatting her away.

"Hey!" Darryl shouted. "How dare you hit her? She's my girlfriend!"

Darryl zoomed in and tore the book from my grasp, sending it flying across the room. I swung around, but Gerald and I were completely surrounded.

"What now?" Gerald asked.

"Um, do you have another good book?" I suggested.

"Well, *The Lord of the Flies* is pretty interesting…"

"Hardcover! For swatting with!"

"Oh, right."

Just then, Sally came zooming at me.

"Oooohhh, am I going to let you have it!" she roared. "No one smacks me and gets away with it!"

But before she could sting me, something struck her and she went flying into the wall. I turned, and there stood Jeannine, book in hand.

"Jeannine! I told you to stay where it's safe!"

"Shut up, Will! I'm saving you!"

It's kind of hard to argue with her when she gets stubborn like that.

"Fine!" I growled. "But you've got the book now. What can I use to fight them off?"

"Here!" She tossed something at me.

"A *pillow*? Seriously?"

"Beggars can't be choosers," Jeannine admonished.

At that moment, surrounded by an attacking horde of giant bees, it seemed like a bad time to tell her how my last attempt at using a pillow for a weapon had turned out, so I took it and began swinging.

"Turn around!" I said to her. "I'll guard your back and you guard mine."

"Fine!" Jeannine said, spinning around until we were back to back. "If you think you're up to it!"

157

"I'm up to it!" I shouted, then turned to Gerald. "Gerald! It all comes down to *you* now! We'll fend off the bees while you get the RevealeR! Go!"

"I'm on it!" Gerald said. Then he made a mad dash for the desk.

In all fairness, he came pretty close. As Jeannine and I smacked and swatted away, he made it as far as the desk, and began to reach under. Unfortunately, a few bees broke off from the group that Jeannine and I were battling and followed Gerald. As he stretched and strained to reach the RevealeR, they wrapped their spindly appendages around his legs and pulled him away from the desk. More bees then flew in and grabbed his arms as well.

"Bring him to me," the King Bee commanded. "Finish the others."

"No!" Gerald cried. "Stop! Leave my friends alone!"

"You can't help them," the King Bee cackled as Gerald was dragged before him. "You can't help anyone."

Gerald glared at him with burning hatred in his eyes. He stiffened his feet and pulled himself free, but the King Bee just laughed at him.

"Come, fight me," the monster challenged. "No? Of course you can't! You're weak. You're a nameless, faceless bug. And you'll spend the rest of your life serving me!" And then he laughed some more. Gerald, though no longer held by the bees, pulled at his arms as though he was still restrained. He wavered.

"Look at me," the King Bee commanded. "See the face of your master. Then watch how these fools suffer for defending you."

Gerald gasped, "No," but then stared in horror as the bees attacked me and Jeannine. He whimpered, but then his head slumped, and turned away.

"What's the matter?" the monster taunted. "Can't stand to face the terrible truth?"

"Um, Gerald?" Jeannine cried out as she continued swinging the book desperately, each swipe getting lower and slower. "We could use some help right about now!"

She was *so* right. Both of us were clearly running out of gas, and the bees, sensing our weakness, snickered, and drew in closer. My pillow had burst in several places, and floating feathers formed a halo around my head. I waved what was left of the pillow around, but it wasn't much of a defense. One bee flew right through the casing and stung me on the thigh. I fell back and tried to remain upright, but another bee stung me on my knee, and I collapsed.

Without me to protect her back, Jeannine was quickly overwhelmed.

"Ahhhhhhh!" she cried as she was stung in several places at once. She fell beside me, and the monsters rose above us.

"I... I'm sorry, Jeannine," I whispered hoarsely as I tried to roll toward her. Jeannine remained on her back, staring up at the bees as they rose above us.

"Gerald..." she whispered. Gerald's eyes, coated with bitter tears, rose to her reflexively. "Gerald, help us..."

But Gerald did not answer her plea. He pressed his eyes shut, but could not close them tightly enough to hold back his tears. As he wept, the tips of a dozen daggers slowly descended on Jeannine and me. The monsters took their time, enjoying our anguish and helplessness.

"You must watch this, Gerald," the King Bee commanded. "See the penalty for defying me."

Suddenly, Gerald's eyes flew open wide, and he spun his head, searching frantically.

"Aha!" he whispered, then sprang over to the table and picked up the cigarette lighter. He flicked the lighter, which sparked, but did not ignite. As he struggled with it, scores of gleaming stingers closed in. Serrated daggers were within inches of our heads.

"Come ON!" he growled desperately.

At that very moment, one of the sparks from Gerald's lighter finally caught fire, sending flame out of the tip. The bees all looked at him and laughed heartily.

"You think that itty-bitty fire can hurt us?" the King Bee snickered. Surprisingly, Gerald smiled.

"It's not for *you*," he said, and then turned to the desk. When he turned back, there was something in his other hand. He held it up for the monster to see.

160

"The bracelet?" the monster croaked. "What are you doing with that?"

"What I should have done a long time ago," Gerald replied. Then he took the bracelet and held it to the flame.

"No!" the monster cried. "Noooooo! Don't…"

But before he could finish another word, the bracelet caught fire. The flame quickly rose high into the air, flaring like an acetylene torch. The King Bee screamed as the powerful rays scorched him. He flailed, and swung at Gerald to no avail. The fire filled the room with the brightness of a supernova, which consumed the king and all the bees surrounding him, shriveling them like paper in a fireplace.

"Uh, Sally, is it warm in here?" Darryl asked.

"Shut up you idiot!" said Sally. Then they both burst into flame. All of the bees squirmed and squealed as they burned, until finally, like the bracelet itself, they turned to ashes. Gerald dropped the burning embers into his trashcan as the darkness, at last, fled the room.

"Good riddance," he said to the smoldering ashes.

Jeannine and I sat up. We stretched, and inspected our wounds, but then began brushing ash off of our clothes.

"Are you guys okay?" Gerald asked.

My body hurt like I had been used as a football tackling dummy, but I gave him a painful thumbs-up. Jeannine moaned a bit, but did the same.

"I did it, guys!" Gerald smiled, straightening himself proudly. "I defeated the monster!"

Jeannine and I both smiled back our approval, though those smiles turned to grimaces as we struggled to our feet. I looked around, surveying the damage. With the monsters gone, the room had returned to normal: it was filled with a midnight blue haze that filtered in through the window, but the unnatural shadows and murky fog had retreated. The shredded mosquito netting and pillows were strewn across the floor, and there were still feathers in the air that were drifting lazily to the ground. Thankfully, the pain and the nasty welts from the bee stings faded once the monsters that inflicted them had been vaporized.

"Well, Gerald Hoffsteadtler," Jeannine applauded. "It seems you're a full-fledged hero now. Congratulations!"

"Thanks," Gerald said. "You were pretty good at saving the day yourself."

"Yeah, thanks Jeannine," I echoed. "This is getting to be kind of a habit with you: charging in and saving the day. But how did you know to come bursting in at just that moment? How did you know what was going on in here?"

"I've been sitting at the door all night, listening to you two."

"But you said you would *leave*," I recalled.

"You asked me to go," she reminded. "You didn't say how far."

I couldn't help smiling at her.

"You did good, Jeannine," I said. "Thanks. I... *we* couldn't have done it without you."

"Yeah, thanks," echoed Gerald. "And Will...I, um... Look, I'm sorry about that whole ketchup bomb in your locker thing."

"That was *you*?" I sputtered. "You exploded ketchup packets in my locker?"

"Well, it wasn't *me* exactly," he mumbled meekly. "I was just kind of an advisor. I mean it's not like J.T. or any of those other meatheads could figure out how to do something like that on their own."

Jeannine started giggling.

"It's not funny!" I barked.

162

"Look," Gerald said. "Let me make it up to you."

"Fine!" I said crossly. "You can start by paying up!"

"You can start," Jeannine said diplomatically, "with a nice bowl of ice cream. I'm in the mood for a treat. Aren't you, Will?"

"Yeah, right. Whatever," I mumbled. "Just give me a minute. I'll catch up."

But as Gerald and Jeannine walked out the door, I called to her.

"Just make sure that the syrup is real chocolate!" I yelled as the door closed behind them.

And then I slumped back down, alone in Gerald's darkened room.

Chapter 12 - Reversals

It's a pretty sad day when neither triumphing over monsters nor the thought of a well-deserved bowl of ice cream can snuff the lingering gloom engulfing you. But even though we had solved the case, I didn't feel much like celebrating. I held up my flashlight, which was still cold and lifeless, and pouted.

"Where can it be?" I asked myself. "How will I ever find the source of my powers?"

The misery clinging to me darkened the atmosphere wherever I moved. Darkened it so much, in fact, that I didn't even notice that someone else had entered the room.

"Don't worry, Will. It will all work out."

I spun around, and there was Jeannine. She must have slipped quietly back in, because I hadn't heard her enter. She came and sat before me.

"What, no ice cream for you after all?" I asked.

"Come on, Will," she said, patting my hands sympathetically. "Don't be so down on yourself. So what if you needed help? You know I'll always be there for you."

"Thanks, partner." I looked up at her and smiled weakly. Jeannine returned the smile, but it was strangely twisted, and her eyes were not as warm as the words she spoke.

"And you, Will?" she murmured, drawing closer. "Will you always be there for *me*?"

"Well, sure," I mumbled awkwardly. "You're my partner, aren't…"

But I stopped speaking. Where she had been patting my hands, her fingers, which were oddly cold, surrounded and grasped mine. She drew near, and I froze like a stone. Her face was closer to mine than it had ever been.

"Of course you will," she whispered. "After all, without me, you're all alone, aren't you?"

"Jeannine!" I protested meekly. "What are you doing?"

But she kept coming toward me. Her face leaned back as it approached, and I was as locked in place as a roller coaster rider strapped to the seat. When she was just inches away, her lips began to part.

Suddenly, tiny sparks of light shot through the air above us like an ant-sized Roman Candle. Startled out of my hypnotic trance, I broke contact with Jeannine and scanned for the source.

"Oh, nuts!" I cried out as I searched in vain. "If only I could use my MonsterScope!"

165

I reached into my pocket, but when I pulled out my MonsterScope, it was stone cold, just like the RevealeR. As I growled in frustration and stuffed it back into my pocket, Jeannine came beside me and pressed her hands down on mine.

"Oh, why not let it be?" she said. "It doesn't matter, anyway. Look."

Her eyes pointed mine to the gap between Gerald's desk and wall. There, struggling to rise, pulsed a tiny glowing dot. It floundered in the same spot where the ball of light that erupted from my RevealeR had fallen the day before.

"Poor, hopeless thing," Jeannine uttered casually. "But there's nothing that can be done for it."

The dot of light was fading. I looked at Jeannine, who was once again smiling strangely. A chill ran up my spine. That sixth sense of mine was screaming at me from the back of my head.

"You...you're not really Jeannine, are you?" I said weakly. I pointed my RevealeR at her, but its light was still nowhere to be found.

"What?" she said with a very fake pout. "Why Will, you're being ridiculous now." And she drew closer and wrapped her frigid hands around my arm.

I tried to back away, but she held on tightly, pulling me in. My mind raced like a Ferrari, but with my flashlight and MonsterScope useless, I needed to find some other way to reveal the truth. My panic-driven brainstorm yielded a crazy idea.

"Yes, I *am* ridiculous," I conceded. "I'm ridiculous. And hard-headed. And even cranky sometimes. But *you* are a nag, Jeannine. The worst nag on the face of the Earth."

Jeannine smiled, and cooed, "Oh Will, you say the cutest things." Then she drew closer, her arms wrapping my chest tightly as her face approached my shoulder.

Well, if I had wanted proof that this wasn't really Jeannine, that was more than enough. The real Jeannine would have bitten my head off for that remark more fiercely than any monster ever could.

"You make me feel so safe, Will," she said as she snuggled into the crease of my neck. The tight squeeze of her arms grew painful as they wrapped like vines around me, and her breath, where it fell against my ear, felt like icy daggers. I scanned the room desperately for anything I could use to defend myself. My eyes caught sight of the flickering dot of light, fading quickly into nothingness, as the vine-like arms grew ever tighter, squeezing the air from my lungs. Even though the light was well out of reach, its warmth braced me against the cold engulfing my body.

Something about that speck is so familiar, I thought. Right then, my gaze was drawn to the pictures on Gerald's wall, the ones that had been uncovered when he tore down his James Dean poster. In the center, mounted on the most worn, handmade frame of the lot, was a drawing of a boy flying through the air. He wore green rags for clothes and a hat with a feather in it, and was holding a wooden flute in his hand. Hovering beside him was a bright speck of light.

"A fairy," I whispered.

"What did you say?" cried Jeannine, recoiling in horror. I looked her right in the eye and said, "The glowing dot is a fairy. But you already knew that, didn't you?"

"No! Noooooo!" she howled. "You don't know what you're saying! You can't mean that!" But I persisted.

"I understand now," I said. "I don't need my RevealeR to see you for what you really are."

Jeannine screeched, and her whole body began to writhe. The scream grew into a low howl as she shook and twisted. Finally, her face melted, revealing another form underneath. As its Jeannine-mask dripped away, a black, three-corner hat with a skull insignia spread across the monster's brow. Below that draped a red, silver-buckled jacket with a bronze cutlass tucked into its belt. One of its sleeves was empty, but for the gleam of a silver crescent glistening within. I smiled.

"Captain Hook, I presume?" I said.

"Aye," the monster cackled. "An' what be you? Another o' Pan's Lost Boys?"

"No, I'm a monster detective!" I said proudly.

"Oh, are ye now? Well, no matter. I'll make short work o' ye!" Then he pulled the sword from his belt and raised his arm to strike. As he swung the blade, I parried with my RevealeR and deflected the blow.

"Fool! Blackguard!" he roared, "Ye've got no sword!" The monster drew back his sword for another thrust. "Yer powerless against me, ye foolish child!"

"So what?" I answered. "That's never stopped me before!" But my flashlight was too short to block the next swing, and the blade cut right through the upper sleeve of my jacket. A searing pain shot through my arm, and I knew that Hook was right: I needed a weapon. I needed *light*. But the only source of light was…

I looked back at the fading speck.

Come on, Will! You've read Peter Pan. I thought furiously. *What is it that revives fairies?*

But right then, another thrust of the monster's cutlass distracted me. I dove into the desk to dodge it, crashing, as always, on my head. The pain throbbed so bad that it felt like someone was inflating a giant balloon inside my temples. As I struggled to right myself, the monster cornered me and raised his gleaming sword.

168

"I got ye now," he hissed gleefully. "Did ye think ye could escape me f'rever?"

But that rap on the head must have shaken loose my memory, because at that very moment the answer came to me.

"I believe in fairies," I cried out.

"What?" the monster growled. "What did ye say?"

"I believe in fairies," I shouted. "I do!"

Instantly, sparkles shot into the air from the floor by the desk. The floundering speck of light arose from where it had fallen and soared, growing bright and strong. As it zoomed to my side, warmth filled me, spreading from deep within my chest to the tips of my fingers. Soothing and radiant, it was an island of comfort in a sea of darkness. Meanwhile, Captain Hook moved to strike once more, but the tiny glowing ball circled the monster, darting back and forth around his head.

"Stop, ye fool!" the pirate cried. "This can't save ye!"

"I believe in fairies!" I shouted. "I do!"

He swung wildly at the flying speck, but the light dodged artfully.

"I'll get ye!" the monster roared. "Yer no match fer me!"

But as his mouth yawned wide to shout, the ball of light took advantage of the opening and flew down his throat.

"No! No! Yearrgh..." he gagged as he swung around wildly. His attack crumbled, and his form swayed and began to shake. Captain Hook staggered and stumbled, holding his throat as though he was suffocating. Finally, his shirt burst open and his body cracked like an egg. Powerful rays poured out of the fissures, which grew wider as the form containing them fell away.

"Hah!" I cheered. "That'll show you! When will you monsters ever learn that light always triumphs over..."

But I cut myself off mid-sentence. Something was very

169

wrong. As the monster fell apart and disappeared in a burst of light, something arose from out of the depths of the darkness behind him: something that must have been there all along, hiding. Something dreadful. Deep in the shadows, its form grew, bleeding all of the light from the air surrounding it. Even from across the room, the brutal cold it radiated pierced me.

"The Hidden Beast," I whispered.

As the light that had burst forth from the vanquished pirate-monster faded, the form of the monster lurking behind him became clear. My eyes widened in shock as a voice, soaked in impatience and scorn, called to me.

"Will! What nonsense are you up to now?"

"Oh... Oh, NO!" I gasped. "Not *YOU*..."

This monster had no claws, no fangs, no bat-like wings. It didn't breath fire or shoot acid, and this was one monster that would never tolerate slime spewing all over the place. Its only weapons were a dust rag, spray bottle of glass cleaner, and a dreadful look of exasperation.

"*MOM?*"

"Playing childish pretend games...*again*?" she hissed.

"M-mom," I stuttered. "I...I'm sorry..."

"Oh for heaven's sake, Will," huffed the monster version of my mother. "Just look at what's become of you – you're a mess!" And faster than I could blink, she was upon me, fussing over my hair, straightening my hat, and brushing off my jacket with her cloth. But instead of cleaning it, her rag turned my coat black, as though she was brushing on shadows with a paintbrush. Her touch stung like icy needles, and the creeping darkness that she was covering me with crawled on my skin like frozen ants. I broke away and tried to steady myself, but tremors took root in my knees and began to spread.

"What…what happened to my fairy?" I whispered as my head spun back and forth.

"Your *fairy*?" my mother scoffed, straightening up and putting her hands on her hips in her classic '*You are in SUCH trouble*' pose. "Really? You're searching for a fairy? Next thing you know, you'll tell me you're looking for Santa Claus."

I stumbled back. As I withdrew, she turned her hand up, and all of the scattered filth in the room, the dirt, the grime, and even the dust bunnies, arose. The air grew murky, and then the monster pointed in my direction, and the dark mists swirled around me as though a squall was whipping them into a frenzy. I searched in vain for the light. For *any* light.

"It's not like that."

"Well, what silly fantasy is it this time, Will? Are you Peter Pan fighting Captain Hook? Sherlock Holmes battling Professor Moriarty? Or are you a secret agent conquering space invaders?"

"N-no, this is *real*," I insisted as I fought to steady myself against the smoky whirlwind attacking me. "I fight monsters. I save people."

"Ridiculous make-believe delusions! Acting the hero? Fighting evil? Saving the day? You're just a little boy with a big imagination!"

The air grew so thick and heavy that I gagged on it.

"I do good," I whispered hoarsely. "Fight for truth…"

"Fight for truth? What utter rubbish! In the real world, do you know what we call people who believe in foolish things like that? Crackpots. Tattletales. Heretics. And everyone hates them."

"S-stop. Please…" I wheezed as waves of shadowy mist filled my lungs, drowning me.

"No, *you* stop," she hissed gleefully, "You've got to grow up, Will. Tell me that you're going to give up all of this silly nonsense and I can release you. Then you can be free."

My sight faded, and my limbs stiffened from the icy darkness that was pouring into my body. I stumbled to my knees.

"N-no," I gasped.

As I struggled for breath, frigid numbness marched toward my heart. A warm glow from deep within – the warmth that filled me when I revived the fairy – slowed the bitter flood, but could not hold it back. As the cold penetrated deeper and I began to shiver, a voice rang out from the back of my mind.

Find the source, Will.

In that moment, as darkness overtook me and I fell to the floor, I knew. Somehow, I think I had always known. In the instant before I succumbed, I made my choice – knowing that it could possibly be the last choice I would ever make.

"I...I..." I choked out, "I...believe...in fairies."

"What?" my mother sneered. "No! That's crazy!"

But I struggled back to my knees, and rose to face her.

"It is not crazy," I wheezed defiantly. "It's truth. *My* truth. I believe that. I'm going to go on believing it. And nothing you do or say will change that."

A horrible wail erupted from my monster-mother.

"Nooooooo!" she cried. "You must stop! You must put an end to this nonsense!"

"I will not!" I called out even as I gasped for air. As I did, the warmth within me swelled. I coughed, but then raised my head high and announced, "You call it nonsense, but I know what I've seen. And I know what I believe."

The fever in me blossomed so intensely that I began to

glow. *Really* glow. An overpowering brightness flowed from my body, almost as if I were a fairy myself. Darkness fled my lungs, and the misty shadows retreated back to their master.

"I believe!" I shouted boldly. "I believe in fighting for truth and justice!" As my words grew louder, the light radiating from me grew stronger, and the monster, as monsters do, cringed and shrank.

"Stop! You can't...." it pleaded.

"I believe in defending the weak, and standing up for what's right," I continued. "I believe in bravery and heroism!"

The room grew bright as the dawn, but the monster, though diminished and cowering, still fought to send its dark tendrils to attack. But the radiance pouring out of me, growing brighter and stronger, drove them back.

"And I believe in the power of truth and understanding. I believe in trust and loyalty. And I believe in forgiveness. But most of all," I announced, "Most of all, I believe in LIGHT!"

And with that, the outpouring of light came together and congealed into a luminous fireball. Churning like a hurricane, it surged through the room, and the monster was swept up in its burning brightness.

"This isn't over! I'll get you!" the monster promised as she was swallowed by the light. "Someday I'll get you! You know I will!"

"I believe in light! It lives! It fills the world!" I shouted as the intense flame melted the shrinking monster to slag. The ball of light, majestic as the sun, circled the room triumphantly, dipping into every nook and crevice, chasing scores of lurking shadows from their dark lairs. Trapped out in the open, they dissolved. The light then flew to the center of the room where it hung for a moment, condensing further until it was about the size of a grape. It glided gently toward me and hovered close to my ear. And then something really amazing happened.

The light spoke to me.

"Thank you, boy of faith, boy of wonder. You do believe in me," the voice, soft as a breeze, confirmed. "And I...I believe in *you*."

And then the light floated to my cheek, which flushed from its warmth. It almost felt like it was giving me a kiss, though thankfully not the wet, slobbery kind that I get from my great aunt Martha. Finally, the glowing ball floated and flittered its way back to my RevealeR, where it flew inside the housing. I flicked the switch, and the beam came on strong.

"Welcome back," I said happily.

I flicked the flashlight off and put it in my pocket. When I checked my other pocket, there was my MonsterScope, its glowing aura restored, as good as new. I thought of the heavy dumbbell that it had turned into and said to myself, "Well, I've definitely been getting plenty of exercise on this case."

I was about to put the glass back in my pocket and follow Jeannine and Gerald downstairs for some ice cream, when I spied a something out of the corner of my eye. A tiny, glimmering object sitting on Gerald's desk seemed to be calling to me. I went over to check it out, my scope raised to my eye.

It was a hook. It had shrunk so small that it almost looked like a picture hanger, but under the gaze of my MonsterScope, it showed itself to be a powerful monster. It was contained now, sleeping perhaps, but I remembered the creature's last words before it succumbed to the light.

I'll get you! the monster promised. *Someday I'll get you! You know I will!*

I shuddered a bit as I remembered. But I also remembered what kept the beast imprisoned. And Bigelow was right, as always: it was there within me all along.

"I believe," I whispered to myself. The hook shook violently in protest. I smiled, and then picked it up and placed it, and my MonsterScope, securely in my pocket. After all, leaving it lying there would have been very untidy. Then I went downstairs for some ice cream.

Chapter 13 - Crownings

The stench of disinfectant stung my nose before I even walked through the door when I got home that night. Let me tell you, the aromas of pine cleaner and chocolate ice cream, the scent of which had followed me all the way from Gerald's kitchen (I had spilled quite a bit on my jacket, you see), do not mix well. My mom was fast asleep on the couch; waiting, as always, for the comforting clatter of the door opening and the thumping sound of my steps as I walked in. She stirred, and groggily raised her head.

"Will?" she called out.

"It's me, mom," I answered softly as I quietly closed the door, shutting out the growing tempest that filled the night sky. A weary smile crossed her lips. She yawned, and then rolled over and pulled the blanket to her shoulders.

"It's good you're home," she sighed. "It's getting stormy out there."

"Yes it is," I agreed as the muted clash of the wind whipping at the foundations echoed around us. But the ticking of the clock in the kitchen rose above those other noises.

I believe in trust.

"Mom, I missed my curfew tonight," I confessed. "I'm sorry, but I got held up at Gerald's house. Our project took longer than I expected."

My mother rolled to face me, and her eyes labored open.

"Did you finish what you needed to do?" she asked drowsily. I nodded.

"I did. But I'll understand if I'm grounded again."

Wearily, but intently, my mother studied me. A cold glint shimmered in the corner of her eyes, but as her gaze lingered, it faded.

"No, that's all right," she sighed. "There's no need to ground you for every little thing."

"What? Who are you, and what did you do with my mother?" I quipped. "You grounded me for three days when I came home late from Timmy Newsome's house."

"Well, I think we can start being a little flexible about your curfew. After all, you're a very responsible boy."

And then she snuggled comfortably into her blanket and drifted back to sleep.

The image that reflected from the mirror when I stopped to clean up startled me. The harsh, stark light of the bathroom fixture revealed features that were familiar, and yet foreign. The differences were slight, but the eyes that stared back at me looked deeper, the skin had grown pale, and the chin appeared firmer. Thankfully though, except for some rips in my already beat-up jacket, all other visible evidence of the night's battles had faded. The welts from the monster-bee stings were gone, though the ache remained. I shrugged, and set about washing off the ice cream stains from my coat.

Maybe it was the aches that weakened me, or the fatigue that came from a night of combat, but the door to my room seemed a lot heavier than normal. As I strained to push it forward, the door resisted. When it finally cracked open, a strange odor overtook me. It smelled like a ballpark: the comforting scent of fresh air, mown grass, hot dogs, and old leather. I sighed.

"You're here, aren't you?" I called into the darkness.

"Yes."

When I flicked the wall switch to turn on the light, there on my bed, munching on stale popcorn as casually as before this adventure began, sat the familiar form of Bigelow Hawkins. He did not speak, which would have pleased my mother, since she always tells me not to talk with my mouth full.

"That bag of popcorn is over a week old," I told him.

"Mmm hmm," Bigelow mumbled as he chewed.

"I dumped the shavings from my pencil sharpener in there."

"What's your point?"

I didn't answer. Instead, I inspected my monster detective mentor carefully. For the most part, he had returned to his usual form: dark, hairy, and sharply clawed under his oversized hat and coat, but I noticed that the stubby little legs hanging over the edge of my bed were dressed in a baggy pair of SpongeBob pajamas.

"Another new look?"

"It's casual Friday," he explained.

"Today is Saturday," I pointed out.

"Not for me it isn't."

And then quiet fell upon us. The silence grew, like the monsters themselves, until it filled the room. And only the words I was chomping at the bit to say could deflate it.

"You didn't answer when I called out for you the other day. Not even a note. I thought maybe you were gone for good."

Bigelow didn't reply. But he did stop chewing.

"Why, Bigelow?" I finally asked. "Why did you abandon me?"

"I didn't. I would never do that, Will."

"I was lost and alone!" I cried. "Where were you?"

"I was here. I was with you the whole time."

"Then why didn't you appear?"

"That," Bigelow said, "was *your* choice."

"What? What are you talking about?"

"You already know the answer."

I squirmed uncomfortably, and began pacing back and forth. Bigelow sat, patient as the ocean, waiting for me to gather my thoughts.

"Was it because I stopped believing in you, like with my RevealeR?" I asked.

Bigelow shook his head. "No. It was because you did not want to hear what I had to say."

I made a sour lemon face, and shook my head.

"Now you sound like my mother," I grumbled. Bigelow smiled that toothy, monster grin of his.

"I'll take that as a compliment," he said. "The simple fact is: I had already told you what you needed to do. You just weren't willing to listen."

I stiffened defensively. My teeth tightened into a grimace, but then slowly I drew deep breaths and steadied.

Finally, my head slowly nodded.

"I had to find the source of my power," I whispered. "No one could do it for me."

"Precisely. You struggled with accepting this truth. That was what prevented you from recognizing and confronting your new monster."

"But how could I have monsters again? I conquered the monster that released all the others. I defeated my Hidden Beast."

Bigelow looked down.

"You defeated one manifestation of it," he finally said. "But the Hidden Beast can never be completely vanquished. It is a constantly growing, ever-changing fiend. You can overcome it, control it for a time, but it will always find a new form to take by finding, deep inside us, the memories, thoughts, and feelings that we retreat from, and grow them until they are formidable foes."

"Like the one that took the form of my mother," I surmised. "The one that wanted me to grow up."

"No," Bigelow corrected. "That is what the monster *said* it wanted. What did it really want?"

"It … it wanted me to feel childish. It wanted me to give up on my values and beliefs."

"Yes. Your most noble values: trust, loyalty, honesty, forgiveness; many will try to convince you that faith in these things is foolish. And yet they are the source of your inner strength. They are the core of all that is good in humanity."

"Faith," I whispered, and once again felt warmth glow within me. "That was what empowered me. It was faith that saved me."

"Yes, faith is an unimaginable power, strong enough to move mountains."

"And that was what helped me refuse to turn my back

on my beliefs," I said proudly, feeling energy surging within me. The RevealeR in my hand burned with contained power. Bigelow nodded.

"You showed great courage tonight, Will. You remained true to yourself, even in the face of darkness. You have once again proven yourself to be a true hero."

I beamed, and Bigelow gave an approving grin.

"But be on guard, Will," he cautioned. "Faith is strong, but it is also fragile. The wrong words can crush it."

And then he pulled his stumpy legs back onto the bed and waved my blanket into the air. By the time it settled back onto my bed, he had vanished once more.

Most of the day Sunday I lazed about the park, spending a lot of the time swinging on the swings, happily flying high through the air. I carried my MonsterScope with me to school the following morning, partly because I was so happy to have it back again, and partly because I was still a bit spooked about the whole monster-Jeannine thing. I know that was part of the reason because I checked her out with it four times on the bus alone. Jeannine was herself of course, but her wardrobe looked like a monster had definitely taken over her closet. Her old combat boots were back on her feet, paired with mismatched striped and polka-dotted socks. The pink jacket was gone, replaced by a tie-dyed vest, beneath which she wore a black, skull-faced t-shirt and a pair of cut-off denim shorts. But the crowning item, in more ways than one, was her hat. It was shaped like a bell, but for the front, where the brim was rolled back along her forehead and down her cheeks, framing her face. Where a hatband might have been, a set of aviator goggles was strapped across instead. It looked kind of like the hat Snoopy wears when he goes off to fight the Red Baron, but for the fact that it was purple and had a big yellow daisy made of lace and satin pasted above the left ear.

"Nice hat," I remarked casually. Jeannine glanced at me suspiciously, then lifted her nose and turned away.

"Thank you." She said. For once, I was grateful for the haughty tone in her voice. This was the Jeannine I knew.

"What, no pink today?" I asked.

"It's not Wednesday. You know that Wednesday is my pink day."

"Yeah, but it's been Wednesday a lot lately."

"Maybe. But I've decided that one Wednesday a week is enough."

At that very moment, a squeal erupted behind us. From a seat several rows back, two girls sprang upon us: Tiffany Wells and her sidekick, Jaime.

"Jeannine!" Tiffany sputtered. "What on Earth have you done to yourself?"

Jeannine batted her eyelashes innocently.

"Whatever do you mean?"

"Your outfit! What is that ghastly thing you're wearing on your head?"

"It's a hat. Obviously."

"Stylish girls like us don't wear hats! And certainly not atrocious ones like that! Do we, Jaime?"

The pale, dark-haired girl trailing her said nothing, but kept stealing glances at me, looking away every time I spotted her doing it.

"Clearly," Jeannine replied loftily, "some of us *do*."

"Oh really?" Tiffany's face scrunched like she had sucked on a lemon. "There wasn't a single person wearing a hat on the red carpet at any of the awards shows, or in the pages of Vogue or Cosmo."

182

"Well, not all of us copy what we see others wear. Some of us think for ourselves."

For a few uncomfortable moments, Jeannine and Tiffany glared at each other, but then Tiffany broke eye contact and withdrew.

"Humpf! Come on, Jaime! Let's go." And the two of them retreated to the back of the bus.

"The nerve of her!" Jeannine hissed. "Thinking she can pass judgment on what I wear!"

"Well, in all fairness," I commented, "It's not exactly fashionable."

"This from the boy who wears a Salvation Army Store trench coat, and doesn't know a bowler hat from a Fedora."

"Well, call it what you want, but I know what I like."

"So then tell me: what do YOU think of the hat?"

I tilted my head back and forth, studying Jeannine from every angle. To be perfectly honest, I purposely took an extra-long time checking her out, just to keep her in suspense.

"It's you," I finally said with a smile.

Jeannine beamed. "It is, isn't it!" she said brightly.

And then we settled comfortably into our seats for the rest of the trip to school.

The rest of the morning was generally uneventful, though there was one incident that was extremely gratifying to witness. It occurred in science class, when J.T. Anderson got a stern talking to from Mr. Stines about his latest assignment.

"Seriously, Mr. S.," J.T. flustered, "I was going to work on my project with my…ah, *tutor* on Sunday. But he blew me off. Said something about…"

"It is not your tutor's responsibility to do your work, Mr. Anderson!" Mr. Stines bellowed loudly. "It's yours!

You will present your assignment to me, done by your own hand, first thing tomorrow, or I will be on the phone with your parents. Is that clear?"

J.T. cowered. "Y-yes sir," he replied meekly.

"Good! Now sit up straight and get to work!"

J.T. bent over his desk and lowered his head. When his hair drooped forward, I noticed with great satisfaction that his exposed forehead was covered with lots of blotchy red pimples. J.T.'s eyes shot furtive glances left and right to see if anyone was watching, then he pulled a pair of thick, horn-rimmed glasses from his pocket and quickly slapped them on his face. He guarded them with one hand, and then opened his notebook and began writing. And I thought to myself that what my dad always tells me is true: the world's not fair.

But at certain times, just for a moment, it can come pretty close.

When I entered the lunch room that morning, I spotted Jeannine, once again surrounded by that pink girl-group she was friends with. But from what I could see, the conversation was anything but friendly. Jeannine and Tiffany were exchanging heated words, and Tiffany's flunkies, who were lined up behind her, chimed in too. The one closest to Tiffany, who had a dour expression engraved on her face, was wearing pearl-drop earrings. She pointed and gestured as wildly as a guest on the Jerry Springer Show when she spoke, and the grating whine of her voice made dogs howl in neighboring counties.

"Gerald was right," I whispered to myself. "She IS worse in real life."

The argument grew more animated, but then finally Jeannine gave a huff, spun on her heels, and walked off. The vicious fury in her eyes reminded me once more of that horrible monster-Jeannine. Later, when I sat down at the lunch table next to her, I pulled out my 'scope and checked her out again, just to be sure.

"Would you stop that!" Jeannine said irritably. "What's with you today?"

I looked up at her, fixing me with that impatient Jeannine stare of hers, and thought, *that's my Jeannine all right*! I smiled at her in spite of the scowl she fixed on me.

"Don't ever change, Jeannine," I said to her.

"Humph! Easy for you to say," she grumbled, and then opened her lunch box and started unwrapping her meal.

"Oh no!" she cried out. "Oh, please, not this!"

"What is it?" I said, dropping my smile and lifting my spyglass. "What wrong? Is there a...*something bad* in there?"

"Oh, hush!" Jeannine said, slamming her lunch box shut. "It's just that my mother did it again: tofu, green beans, and carrots for lunch. Sometimes I wish I could buy my lunch from the cafeteria like everybody else."

For safety's sake, I scanned her lunch box with the MonsterScope.

"Well, if it makes you feel any better..."

"It doesn't!" she snapped. "And what's with you and the spyglass today? Are you on a case?"

Should I tell her? I wondered. *Should I tell her about the other Jeannine?*

Jeannine glowered at me, but deep in her eyes was the same uncertainty and doubt that had filled mine all morning each time I looked at her.

I believe in loyalty.

No, I resolved. *That was a monster. A monster that wanted me to question our friendship. Jeannine doesn't deserve to be saddled with that.*

And right then I vowed to never, ever tell her about

what happened after she left the room that night at Gerald's house, to never tell her about the monster-Jeannine that tried to strangle the life out of me.

"No," I answered. "Just testing out my 'scope, now that it's working again."

"Well, point it somewhere else," she insisted, as she turned and went back to rather unhappily peeling the wrappings off her lunch.

"Come on," I said cheerfully. "I'll share my chips with you. And you can have half of my sandwich too."

Jeannine stared at me. It took longer than it should have, but eventually a smile spread across her face. Then she turned her nose up as she scanned the rest of my meal.

"What, no dessert?" she inquired.

"Sorry, no," I apologized. "I'm fresh out of..."

"Chocolate chip cookies, anyone?" a voice from behind us called out. Jeannine and I spun around together.

"Timmy?" I sputtered. "Timmy Newsome?"

And he wasn't alone. Beside him were Rhonda and Gerald. They were standing beside us holding empty trays.

"What are you doing here?" I asked. Timmy didn't answer, but instead turned to Gerald.

"We were wondering if we might join you here," Gerald said. "There seems to be plenty of room. Do you mind?"

I glared at him suspiciously.

"What gives?" I growled. Gerald gulped, then shifted his gaze to Jeannine.

"You didn't tell him?" he asked her.

"Tell me what?" I was starting to feel my cheeks burn, but Jeannine settled me down.

"We talked in the kitchen Saturday night while you were still in Gerald's room. I told Gerald what I wanted as my share of the fee for our services."

"And what was that?" I asked.

"This," Jeannine said, waving her hands at our assembled guests dramatically. "I think that after all we've done...all *you've* done, you deserve some appreciation."

I gaped at her, feeling utterly flabbergasted. Then I turned back to Gerald.

"And you went along with that?" I barked. "What would Tiffany say?"

Gerald blanched. He gave a little cough, and then cleared his throat.

"Yes, well," he mumbled. "Tiff and me are sort of on a break. So, since I'm not hanging with her, I've been thinking about who my real friends are. You and Jeannine stood up for me, even though I didn't make it easy for you. And I guess I still owe you for that ketchup bomb in your locker..."

The mention of that set all of them giggling

"Does *everyone* know about that?" I grumbled. I looked at Jeannine, and she nodded.

"So, anyway, Jeannine suggested that I make up for it by being...well, friendlier. So here I am."

"And me!" Timmy chimed in. "And I brought cookies!"

"And I baked some brownies," Rhonda added, smiling at me shyly. Gerald grimaced, and looked down.

"Um, I didn't bring anything," he said glumly. "But I... I'm *here*. Is that okay with you?"

I believe in forgiveness.

I gazed at them all, standing before me, waiting for me to give the word. I was speechless.

Well, almost.

"Yeah, sure!" I bubbled, sounding so disgustingly cheerful that I practically didn't recognize my own voice. "Why don't you all sit down?"

"Thanks," Gerald said, exhaling loudly. "Just give me a minute and I'll be right back. I have to go over to the cafeteria and buy my lunch."

"Us too," Timmy chimed. And then the three of them turned and headed for the lunch line.

"Oh, okay," I said. "Oh, and Rhonda, you...you look very pretty in that green...um..."

"*Tunic*," Jeannine whispered.

"...tunic you're wearing today."

Rhonda blushed. I looked over at Jeannine, and she gave me a big thumbs up. I thought a moment, and then turned and called out to the others as they left. "Hey! Can you guys chip in for some extra fries for Jeannine?"

"Sure!" Timmy said, looking back and winking at Jeannine. "It'll be my pleasure."

Jeannine smiled bashfully at Timmy, but then her gaze fell from him back to me. When she saw that I was staring at her, she gave me a quizzical look.

"What?"

"Thanks, Jeannine," I said. "For all of this."

She blushed. "You're welcome, Will."

"Look, I'm sorry I didn't tell you about that whole ketchup in the locker thing. I…well, it was pretty embarrassing, and I didn't want to talk about it."

"Oh, that's okay. I'm just glad that you're in a better mood now," she said happily, and smiled. I just looked at her, smiling her patented Jeannine smile at me, and I couldn't help smiling back. Those Jeannine smiles of hers always do that to me.

"Hey, Jeannine, watch this!" I suddenly said.

I took a mouthful of my mashed cauliflower and smushed it out between my teeth. Jeannine tried to hold it in, but a fit of the giggles burst out of her. I joined her in laughter, because Jeannine's laugh has that effect on me too. Still, she was shaking her head when she turned back to her lunch box and opened it once more.

"Oh, Will," she said exasperatedly, though still with some giggle in her voice, "you're never going to grow up."

My laughter stuck in my throat. I thought of the monster, the hook that now sat locked in a mint box lying tucked away in the top drawer of my desk, waiting.

"If only that were true," I said softly. Then I picked up my sandwich and started eating.

After all, I'm still a growing boy.

Chronicles of the Monster Detective Agency

WILL CONTINUE IN

Will Allen
and the
UNCONQUERABLE BEAST

Sherlock Holmes had his Moriarty, Perseus had his Medusa, and King Arthur had his Mordred – and in the next adventure in the Chronicles of the Monster Detective Agency, Will Allen finally comes face to face with his own arch-nemesis: the Lord of Shadows. Only this monster *has* no face!

But how can a monster detective, even one flush with wisdom, strength, and courage, vanquish a horror that cannot be defeated?

TOP SECRET :

CONFIDENTIAL

Tips and Tricks for FIGHTING MONSTERS!

Volume 2

FOR AGENCY RECRUITS
ONLY

To all prospective Monster Detective Agency recruits:

Welcome, and thanks for sticking with us through so many horrors, frustrations, and close calls. We're grateful for your help!

Now, one thing we monster detectives do is look out for each other, so first and foremost, I hope you're staying safe. Remember that you should always speak to a parent or responsible adult before beginning a monster detective adventure.
Remember: they help us stay clear of anything truly dangerous!

The other thing we monster detectives do : we always keep working on improving our detective skills. They're so important for helping us find and conquer the monsters!

I've put in this folder some detective skills-building exercises, puzzles, and questions. Use them to hone your detective eye and sharpen your detective mind. And when you are done with these, you can find some more puzzles left by my Monster Detective friend, Bigelow Hawkins, online at the Monster Detective Agency website, MonsterDetectiveAgency.com. I hope they help!

And don't forget - monsters are only as big as we make them, so be brave and stay strong!

Wishing you confidence and the best of luck,

Will Allen *- Monster Detective Third Class*

MONSTER DETECTIVE AGENCY WORD PUZZLES

Across

3. source of the light of truth

6. Will's new Math teacher

9. Timmy Newsome's tutor

10. the form of Will's 1st monster

Down

1. the Great Monster Detective

2. Will's 1st (unsuccessful) monster bait

4. makes monster tracks visible

5. the deepest, buried fear

7. Jeannine's friends' jacket color

8. Bigelow's fee

```
V W O H M I W V G X L S D C B V O Q Y S
B H O S Y O Z E V I C C I P C B P N Y P
V I I J Y F N Y F I V W T V L K I L G R
P D G C B H H S M G B A V H C Q N D J E
Z D E E E V X R T K B N O L C E K G A V
L E H S L C Y C Y E M X L E Z K X E T E
K N N M Z O R T J I R H H B S Y K Z R A
S B Y L J E W E L N X S U N F P S Z D L
C E O B C T B H A N H F C P J I P Q W E
D A C P H F Z I A M N B G O N C S G Z R
U S R T D F T B D W U Q L G P J Z V M O
M T O M W M H G I A K K M I T E O R J L
K G A N J C M U O A L I O M U K I W E S
E X T O I L E T K U C Z N K X Q M X A L
N H Q O G H C T L O H N Y S K Y Q W N K
E L E Z R X C I F B Z F O Q L J L R N X
C T T E D D Y B E A R L B R K B K G I U
Q J I E D M R S M O S C O W I T Z F N U
U L H L Y P X S C O G F C F T B O E E K
A J X N A L W U C V C H E B F N W Q R Q
```

Once you have figured out all of the crossword puzzle answers, try to find each of them in this word find puzzle!

(Answers on page 197)

MONSTER DETECTIVE LOGIC PUZZLE

Most monsters are tricksters and liars: they feed off of our fears and other bad feelings, so they try to upset us any way they can. But a few, like my friend Bigelow Hawkins, are truth tellers. The trick is telling them apart.

For example, on a recent case I came face-to-face with three ogres. They all had huge fangs sticking out of their mouths, but the first had one big tusk, the second had two, and the third had three. I pulled out my RevealeR to shrink them down – or at least I tried to. You see, my monster-fighting tools can sometime change into different objects, like when my MonsterScope turned into a dumbbell. This time when I reached into my pocket, I pulled out five items: a fog horn, a thermometer, a flyswatter, a pack of tissues, and a key. I placed them all down on the table in front of me.

"Understanding is what powers the RevealeR," I reminded myself. "So if I figure out what form these monsters take, then the object that is really my RevealeR should be empowered, and light up."

But at that very moment, the monsters approached.

"Run away!" roared the one-tusk ogre as he flashed his huge fangs at me. I pooh-poohed him.

"That won't work on me," I scoffed. The three of them turned to each other. The one-tusk ogre threw up his hands, but the other two growled and turned back to me.

"One of us would like to help you," the three-tusk ogre said.

"No we wouldn't!" growled the two-tusk ogre.

"Don't listen to him," said the three-tusk ogre. "The two-tusk ogre always lies."

"That's not true! I do not lie! It is the three-tusk ogre who always lies."

They both turned to the one-tusk ogre, but he only grunted.

"Hmmm," I thought out loud. "I'm going to have to stick around until I figure out which of you is lying."

"Don't stay! You should run and hide!" said the two-tusk ogre. "The three-tusk ogre turns into a giant spider. It's horrifying!"

"No, I turn into the creepy old furnace from the basement. And the two-tusk ogre turns into a ghost ship."

Finally, the one-tusk ogre stepped in and said, "The two-tusk ogre is lying to you. The three-tusk ogre is telling the truth, because he wants to help you."

"No he doesn't!" said the two-tusk ogre. "We all just want to scare you off!"

The three-tusk ogre shook his head. "They are both liars," he said.

All three of them cackled a creepy laugh. But I broke out in a broad smile.

"Well, I may not know everything I need yet," I said as I reached for one of the objects in front of me, "but I do know who is lying and who is telling the truth."

Which object did I reach for, and why?

(Answer on next page)

Logic Puzzle Solution – part I : I reached for the flyswatter. The one-tusk and the three-tusk ogres were the liars, and the two-tusk ogre told the truth. Because he had said that the three-tusk ogre turned into a spider, I thought, "Which of these helps someone deal with spiders?" So I picked up the flyswatter. When I gripped it, it began to glow. Light poured out the end, and then it transformed into my RevealeR. I turned its light on the monsters and they all shrieked, and began to shrink.

"Oh, no," said the three -tusk ogre. "He has figured us out. Now we are lost!"

"No," insisted the two-tusk ogre. "To defeat us, he must deal with Horromungorus, the oldest and strongest one of us, and he does not know how to do that, or which of us that is."

He had a point. The ogres only became a little bit smaller, then they stopped shrinking. Obviously, I needed more information. I tried the direct approach.

"Which one of you is Horromungorus?" I asked.

"I will tell you who is Horromongorus!" called out the one -tusk ogre. "Pick me!"

"Shut up, Fred!" shouted the two-tusk ogre. Then he turned back to me and said, "Only one of us is Horromungorus, and only one of those objects will work on him. The other objects will energize us and make us grow. So if you choose the wrong monster or the wrong object, we will become huge and eat you."

"Why are you telling me all this?" I asked the two-tusk ogre.

"Because sometimes," the monster said with a grin, "there is nothing scarier than truth."

"You must pick the thermometer," said three -tusk ogre. "Otherwise we will eat you."

"No, pick the key," said the one-tusk monster. "That is what you need."

"Didn't I tell you to shut up!" the two-tusk monster growled angrily.

"I know that the other two are liars," I said to the two-tusk ogre. "But you tell the truth. So why don't you tell me what I need to use, and who to use it on?"

The two-tusk ogre's smile grew broad, exposing sharp fangs hidden behind his droopy lips.

"Of course, I will not tell you," he snickered. "I want to see you struggle and squirm while you try to make an impossible decision."

"I want to help!" said the three-tusk monster. "Do not use the tissues on Horromungorus. He will not like it."

"Don't tell him that!" said the one-tusk monster.

"Do not talk to me like I am a baby!" the three-tusk monster growled. "I am the exact same age as Horromungorus!"

"Yes, but I am the oldest," argued the one-tusk monster. "What I say goes!"

"Stop talking!" the two-tusk monster roared. "If you tell him any more, he may figure things out!"

I tapped my finger to my chin as I thought things over, but then smiled and reached for one of the items on the table.

"Unfortunately for all of *you*," I said triumphantly, "I already have."

Which ogre was Horromungorus and which object did I need?

(Answer on page below)

MONSTER OBSERVATION SKILLS PUZZLE
Sharpen Your Detective Eye!

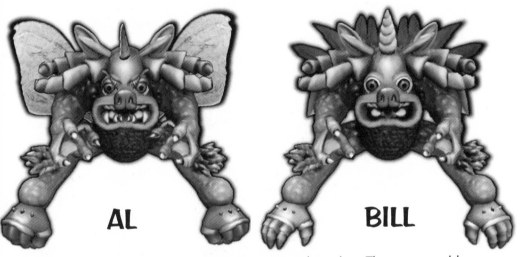

AL   BILL

Little differences are important to a monster detective. They can provide important clues that help us to conquer the monsters and save the day!

Can you identify 6 differences between these two monsters?

(Answers on page 199)

Crossword / Wordfind answers:

Across 3) REVEALER; 6) MRS MOSCOWITZ; 9) JEANNINE; 10) TOILET
Down 1) BIGELOW HAWKINS; 2) ICE CREAM; 4) MONSTERSCOPE; 5) HIDDENBEAST; 7) PINK; 8) TEDDYBEAR

Logic Puzzle Solution – part II

The two-tusk ogre was Horromungorus and the object I needed was the fog horn. Horromungorus was the oldest, and since the one-tusk and three tusk ogres were liars, neither was as old as Horromungorus. And they lied about me needing the thermometer, key, and tissues. Since I was already holding the flyswatter and it was not working on Horromungorus, the fog horn was what I needed.

Needless to say, those monsters were as small as marbles in no time!

MONSTER DETECTIVE REVIEW QUESTIONS

Good memory and reasoning skills are two qualities of a great detective! Below is a series of review questions matched to the **Common Core Literacy Standards** that will ask you to recall key details and practice thinking hard.

A}- Demonstrate understanding of key details.

1. What was Rhonda's HIDDEN BEAST? How was it similar to Gerald's, and how was it different?

2. According to Bigelow Hawkins, what is the source of the RevealeR's power?

3. What character from classic children's literature served as the avatar for Will's first new monster?

4. What features of Gerald's room did Will admire? What does this suggest about Will and Gerald?

5. What item of clothing was Will upset to see Jeannine wearing? Why do you think it disturbed him?

6. What observations clued Will in to the identity of Gerald's monster?

7. What was Will Allen's new HIDDEN BEAST? What event is implied to have set it free?

B}- Recount stories and determine their central message, lesson, or moral.

8. Why do you think light makes the monsters shrink? If light lets us see the truth about things that scare us, would that make monsters more or less scary? Why?

9. What similarities are there in the actions each character had to take to defeat their monsters? What does this imply about dealing with *other* things that might be frightening?

10. What does a person need to do in order to truly see someone else's monster? What can you infer from this to be an important quality for being a good detective?

11. Why did the monsters grow larger and more powerful when Will and his friends tried to escape or hide from them? What does that suggest about running from your fears?

12. Why do you think Gerald's HIDDEN BEAST took the form of a friendship bracelet? What do you think the author is suggesting about the power of peer pressure?

C}- Describe how characters respond to major events and challenges. Explain how their actions contribute to the sequence of events.

13. How did Will Allen react when he first encountered Gerald Hoffsteadtler's monster? How was his reaction different the second time he saw it? What do you think accounted for the change?

14. What does the argument between Will and Gerald on page 130 reveal about them both? What point do you think the author is making? Do you agree?

15. What similarity was there in the way most characters reacted when each of them first saw a monster? Did this reaction help solve the problem, or did they need to develop a new way to respond?

16. Describe Gerald Hoffsteadtler in as much detail as possible, including his appearance, personality, and behavior. Which characteristics do you think best explain why he had a monster?

17. What happens when Gerald confronts the King Bee? What important choice does he ultimately make, and how did that impact both the battle with the monsters and his status afterwards?

18. How did Rhonda's show of gratitude after Will helped to defeat her monster differ from Gerald's? Why do you think it was so different?

D)- Determine the meaning of words and phrases as they are used in a text, distinguishing literal from nonliteral language.

19. What does the word 'friend' mean? How might its meaning be defined differently by Will and Gerald? How might it be defined differently by the King Bee?

20. Why did Will's MonsterScope turn into a dumbbell? What does that suggest about how Will had come to feel about it?

21. What is the name of Will Allen's special flashlight? What does the name suggest about the flashlight's special power?

22. What words did Will and Gerald use to describe the sounds made by Gerald's monster? Why were the words they chose so different?

23. In the story, the feeling of being warm or cold suggested much more than changes in temperature. What might each of those feelings represent?

E}- Describe how a narrator's point of view influences how events are described. Distinguish that point of view from those of other characters.

24. How might Gerald describe Will that is different from the way Will describes himself? What explanation might Gerald have for his unflattering opinion? Is it justified? Why or why not?

25. Will and Gerald had a major disagreement regarding the details of an event that took place in the previous book, *Will Allen and the Hideous Shroud*. How do their remembrances differ? Do you think one of them is recalling the incident more accurately than the other? Why?

26. Do you think Will's feelings influenced how he described certain details in this story? Which ones? What differences might there have been in the story if it was told by Gerald instead of Will?

F}- Compare and contrast the themes, settings, and plots of stories written about the same characters, as well those of others in the same genre.

27. What differences were there between Rhonda's room and Gerald's? How might that account for some of the differences in their monsters? How do both differ from typical monster story settings?

28. If you have read the previous volume, *Will Allen and the Hideous Shroud,* how do the monsters Will Allen faces in that story differ from those in this volume? What changes in Will and his friends might account for some of the differences?

29. How does this Monster Detective story differ from other monster-themed stories you have read?

Additional activities:

30. **Create a monster!** All of the monsters in these stories represent fears or other powerful, negative emotions. Choose one from the list below (or think up one on your own!) and use it as the basis for your creation. Determine what it will look like, sound like, even *smell* like. Where will it come from, and how will it behave?

   A) Envy   B) Jealousy   C) Greed   D) Anger   E) Malice   F) Conceit   G) Rage

31. Bring your creation to life: draw a picture, or make a model with clay or other craft materials. Use your imagination and go wild! Then give it a name. Can you make up a story around your monster?

EXTRA: For FREE teacher's guides & bonus materials, visit our website : http://J81502.wix.com/monsterdetectives

Observation Skills Puzzle Solution :

Bill has no eyebrows, fewer fangs, only 3 fingers, feathers instead of wings, a fat horn, and unclenched feet.

Now, if your detective skills are sharp enough, YOU can be a Monster Detective too! Join us for ...

Help us track down and capture monsters that may be lurking in your local school or library, and earn your own monster detective badge!

Ask a librarian about arranging a hunt, or get info at http://J81502.wix.com/monster-hunt-program